T0062323

Hear Me Angry God

Gerald Kithinji

BOOKLOVE PUBLISHERS

BOOKLOVE PUBLISHERS
P. O. Box 1917, Gweru, Zimbabwe
E-mail:booklove87@yahoo.com

Hear Me Angry God

First published 2016

Editor: E A Makadho
Assistant Editor: Sithabisiwe Sibanda

Copyright © 2016 Gerald Kithinji

All rights reserved. No part of this publication may be reproduced, stored in
a retrieval system or transmitted in any form or by any means, electronic,
mechanical, photocopying, recording, or otherwise, without prior permis-
sion from the publisher.

ISBN   978 0 7974 6468 1

Published in Zimbabwe
by Booklove Publishers
printed by Serveplus Investments
2016

CHAPTER ONE

CULAMAWE

In this sleepy, peasant village set deep in this otherwise vast country, the sun takes longer to rise.

When night falls and the moon is engaged elsewhere, darkness envelops the night right up to the early hours of the next day. Even the first rays of light know that they have a heavy task ahead. They target the early morning stars and dull them with their golden plumes. Then they search for those lone clouds that drag their feet after the leading nimbus clouds have hurriedly climbed the hills and vanished beyond them. Having spread their sharp tongues and touched the ends of the universe, the rays gather courage and smooch the hills of Culamawe, announcing to the dreamy villagers the dawn of a brand new day.

Nonetheless, the villagers choose to wait for the sun to scale the Culamawe Ridge, to the east, and show its fierce face to these remnants of the faded kingdom of Monomotapa, actually Mwenemutapa (the owner of the millet). Then they quickly descend on the arrowroots left over from the previous night's supper and the staple porridge, and are ready for a long, agonising day at the maize fields.

They live on the sweat of their brows, under the increasingly costly protection of their many awesome curandeiros[1].

It is not always easy to distinguish between a genuine witchdoctor, a quack, a wizard, a magician or a sorcerer - but not for these villagers. To them, a genuine curandeiro is all those things rolled into one.

There are those who will charge heavily, and get paid promptly or by instalments. There are those who will charge a paltry sum, and get paid promptly or by instalments. There are no curandeiros who provide relief for charity. Worse still, there are no villagers without an official curandeiro. If

---

[1] Curandeiros - medicine men.

you don't believe it, I will see my own junior curandeiro and he will cure your 'doubting Thomas' syndrome!

If you step on someone's toe, he will not ask you to apologise. He will dare you to step on the other one. Then he will have reason to consult his curandeiro to deal with you perpendicularly. Woe unto you if he should consult the right calibre of a curandeiro! You will have people stepping on your toes every day, and not even having the courtesy to apologise for the inconvenience.

I'm not talking about the type consulted by some government officials in need of promotion. Or by prospectors who want to find diamonds and gold in every shovel-load of soil.

Nor am I talking about the type consulted by a besieged headmaster, who wants to see his deputy fired. Or a director who wants three cars allocated to him and his accountant transferred without lifting his own finger.

I am talking about a real, powerful curandeiro. And a real, powerful curandeiro does not tell you to wash your minibus with detergents, so that it may attract passengers and turn you into a millionaire. He does not give you a concoction to hide in someone's compound in order to make the fellow sick for a week! A mosquito can do that for you.

Take, for instance, the lousy preacher, who took half of his church Sunday collection to a curandeiro for a consultation.

"What is your problem?" the medicine man asked after the preliminaries.

"I am a preacher. But I lack confidence, you know, charisma," the preacher said.

"Charisma? What do you want charisma for?" asked the curandeiro.

"I would like to enter the church and capture the attention of everybody." The preacher gave away his reasons. "When I say 'Hallelujah', I would like the devil and all his spirits to be banished from my presence."

"Ah, I see," the medicine man responded.

"I know you can do that for me. How much will it cost me?" asked the preacher.

"How did you know I could be of help?" the curandeiro enquired.

"The church faithful are well-informed," revealed the preacher.

"I see," noted the curandeiro.

"How much?" the church man asked.

"The church is rich! I can only ask for a fraction. Or what do you say?" the curandeiro asked nonchalantly.

"You are very considerate," observed the client. The preacher opened his briefcase and took out a batch of notes. The curandeiro's mouth was already whet with anticipation.

"Here, this is all I can offer for now," the preacher said as he presented the money.

The curandeiro took the money and proceeded to hide it in his leather bag. He did not count it. It was a gentleman's agreement between two practitioners of different but strict faiths. The curandeiro then resumed his contemplative stance. He appeared to be searching for weighty words for his worthy client. Then he fixed his eyes on the preacher, studying him as if he was a dangerous specimen. The words slowly formed in his mouth.

"It is not enough to believe in your God. You must also believe in yourself. Look at me. Not at my face or neck or mouth. That is not I. Look at my eyes! That's right. You have the potential. But you must tune up those instruments that nature has provided you. Then buy yourself a shiny gold chain. Put it around your neck. Let the congregation marvel at its magnificence. Don't look at the congregation. Look at one of the faithful: there in the middle, there on the side, there at the back. Address that one and address your god. Kneel, kneel!"

The preacher knelt on a mat that his host had spread on the floor.

"Now, chant after me."

"Give me the magic!"

"Give me the magic!"

"Give me the charm!"

"Give me the charm!"

"Give me the power!"

"Give me the power!"

"Give me charisma!"

"Give me charisma!"

The curandeiro then cast the magic spell and offered incantations, and gave the preacher a charm, with instructions that he should never leave the house or enter the church without it.

"If you follow what I have said the congregation will be held captive until you leave."

That was not a serious curandeiro! A real powerful curandeiro keeps you and your people alive. He kills your enemies, if necessary. Not people you don't like or that you hate, but real enemies, real threats to your life or the life of a close member of your family or property. You pay him dearly, because he is lethal. He holds the key to life and death. He kills your enemy's cows or goats or chickens. He is a contract killer with a difference; the difference being that he does not himself touch them. Nor does he send other people to kill them. He uses his powers, supernatural powers!

Have you ever talked to a serious war veteran, an ex-combatente[2]? I mean a soldier who spent many years at the battlefront during the state of internecine strife? It was not merely his skill and luck that kept him alive. He did not survive because he prayed fervently to God. No, he had engaged the services of a serious curandeiro. His chiefs had also consulted serious curandeiros. That is why enemy bullets were ricocheting and killing or wounding enemy soldiers. That is why enemy soldiers were panicking and opening fire on each other. And that is why peace came at last: to avoid total annihilation of all the fighting forces. A serious curandeiro will tell you that.

Without the input of several serious curandeiros, the war would not have deteriorated into a national catastrophe and gone on for so many years. Many idlers and peddlers of hatred believed this.

But the villagers of Culamawe do not have such powerful enemies, like the devil and armed fighters. Their real enemies are poverty, ignorance and disease. The imaginary ones are themselves. They are captives of a vicious cycle of hardship. Poverty and ignorance cannot prevent or cure disease. Ignorance and disease cannot fight poverty: they are on the same side. Disease cannot fight ignorance for the simple reason that one is the flipside of the

---

[2] ex-combatente - a Portuguese term for ex-combatant.

4

other. They go hand in hand. For the villagers of Culamawe, the cure for all these maladies is a real, powerful curandeiro!

Christianity has been here for over three hundred years. But it has not weakened the role of the curandeiro. In some cases, it has strengthened the office of the curandeiro. The curandeiro is, in the majority of cases, a Christian by name.

In Culamawe, there is no winter, autumn or spring. The sun is always there, above their heads at midday. Even when the rains come, which is not often, the sun is there behind the clouds, warming them, turning Culamawe into a hot, humid, sometimes torrid and sodden and dreary place.

The mosquitoes conquered this land a thousand years ago and made it their territory. They grudgingly allow the inhabitants to dwell on it, persistently pursuing them and driving them in droves to their beds, their curandeiros and oftentimes to their deaths.

Their lives revolve around the village headman as well. He is the government's messenger, a privileged one at that and a junior justice of the peace. He keeps the secrets of the government at the local level and occasionally, selectively pulls out a dossier and releases it, usually at a gathering of the village, the convening of which is incumbent on him.

Pinto Junior Madeira once announced at such a meeting the coming of the rains with effect, he said, from the following week. But the rain chose to differ: it came in torrents the very next day and did not stop for two weeks. According to Pinto Junior Madeira, that rain was not official.

The civil war had ended, but suspicion was high on the social ladder, thanks in part to the malicious humming of the pessimists. An official document was therefore necessary for the carrying out of all manner of ordinary chores, whenever the participants were likely to constitute a crowd. The headman spent a large portion of his decision-making time issuing out those documents. A great deal of his time was also devoted to visiting bereaved families and consoling them on his own behalf and on behalf of the government. So hectic was his day that he rarely had his meals at his home. Wherever lunchtime found him that was his home for purposes of lunch. That was his luck and privilege. He worked hard, but the odds and the times were against him.

Had he any contacts with the curandeiros?

Inevitably, for how many other party stalwarts were eyeing a position such as his! He had to protect himself against such misplaced and unwelcome ambition and its bearers. His curandeiro was a master in political medicine!

* * * * * * * * *

Dona Rosa Vanga was a troubled woman until recently when her son, through the services of a curandeiro, relieved her of her misery.

Her husband, Eugenio Vanga Fato, had served the first administration after independence as a soldier. Five years afterwards, he had contracted a disease, which the doctors at the government district hospital could not tame. As a result, he had opted for early retirement, and had settled in Culamawe together with his wife and three young sons. They were Araujo Junior Vanga, Gaspar Eugenio Vanga and Benito Fato Vanga.

His curandeiro, popularly known as Matacanha, was a consummate magician. He kept him alive for two good years, oscillating between life and death. His gratuity and pension formed a significant portion of Matacanha's income. In fact, Matacanha felt the loss of Eugenio Vanga Fato more than anyone else outside the family.

No sooner had she buried her husband than her second son, Gaspar, developed abdominal pains and convulsions, which robbed him of his faculties and strength. The curandeiro gave such treatment as he could, but the problems appeared to mutate and spread to the chest and head. Coughing and intermittent breathing eventually grounded the young man. She had to hunt for another, more powerful medicine man. That cost more money, but she knew the value of good health, so she paid. The treatment kept the young man going for some months and then he relapsed. She even tried some conventional medicine, but that only gave temporary relative comfort.

Then, one fine morning he asked to be moved outside under a tree shade and requested his mother to make some warm millet porridge. He ate a little of the porridge. Then he asked for some chicken soup. His younger brother, Benito, chased and caught a hen, and the soup was eventually presented to

Gaspar. Everybody in the home felt as though he was coming back to them. But late that night he died before her nervous, unbelieving eyes.

Death and gloom again enveloped Dona Rosa's life, leaving her bereft of any vitality for continuation. But this malaise slowly abated and life almost returned to normal.

Her eldest son, Araujo, decided that it was time for him to provide a helper for her. He took in a wife, Maria da Silva, a very attractive woman. From the very beginning, she became a close companion of Dona Rosa.

When several months later she became pregnant, the old lady decided that it was time to see a serious curandeiro for the purpose of protecting the pregnancy and the prospective issue.

"It is vitally important that we should be vigilant," she told Maria. "Anything short of seeing one would be tantamount to gross irresponsibility."

"But I do not know any curandeiros here," she protested. "Why not talk to my husband?"

"Don't be ridiculous!" said Dona Rosa. "These things are not for men. I will arrange everything."

And so it transpired that the two women went to see a curandeira[2]. After the preliminaries, which included the payment of the fee, the curandeira had some questions for them.

"How many sisters do you have?" the curandeira asked.

"Two," Maria responded.

"Are they married?" she probed.

"Not yet," she answered.

"How many aunts do you have?" she asked some more.

"Two," she revealed.

"Are their husbands alive?" the curandeira continued her questioning.

"One is; one is not," Maria exposed.

"Are you on bad terms with any of your sisters or aunts?" the curandeira investigated.

"No," Maria said casually.

---

[2] curandeira - a medicine woman.

"Are you in good terms with all of them?" asked the medicine woman.

"Yes," she answered.

"Do you have another man in your life?" she asked some more.

"Only my husband," Maria said.

"How about this other man I see from your past?" she asked curiously.

"That was before I got married," she said.

"And was he happy about your marrying another man?" the curandeira asked.

"I did not love him," she answered coolly.

"But did he love you?" the medicine woman went on with her inquisition.

"I cannot say. I do not know," she said.

"Does your husband have another woman friend?" she continued to interrogate Maria.

"My son does not have another wife!" Dona Rosa interrupted.

"I asked about a woman friend," said the medicine woman.

"I do not know," replied Maria. "I do not think so."

"Do you love him?" the curandeira asked finally.

"Good God!" exclaimed Dona Rosa.

"Yes, very much," said Maria.

Two concoctions were prepared: one to ward off potential women rivals and another, a love potion, for her husband. Maria was instructed where to hide these and asked to return after three months or whenever need be.

Everything went well for two months. Then one nut went loose, then another and then another. When Maria was not feeling dizzy, she was vomiting. When the nausea subsided she had headaches. And when the headaches faded she had coughs - intermittent dry coughs.

The curandeira gave her several prescriptions, including several 'don'ts'. For instance, she was told not to visit any of her relatives; not to receive any of them for an overnight stay; not to eat food prepared by neighbours; not to shake hands with anybody. In fact, she was directed to cut social intercourse to the bare minimum.

Despite these onerous precautions her condition failed to improve to any appreciable level. She hung on there like a pendulum for almost three months.

Then, one day, her mother visited her and, shocked to see her condition, insisted on taking her to the government hospital two hundred kilometres from there. By the time she got there, she was a pitiable, fragile figure that could hardly stand. The doctor and his nurses fought frantically, but the battle could not be won, not entirely. Maria was saved, but the pregnancy could not. A baby could not be born without a mother; but a mother could have another baby, another time. But that was another matter.

She hung on precariously for two more weeks and then she was on the mend. A month later, she was back at her mother's place, not exactly fit as a fiddle, but a good deal better than expected.

Araujo, who had so far been free of any serious illness, that is, other than malaria, woke up to the fact that he had been scratching himself beyond the normal prickly heat limit. He also noticed that he was having occasional doses of mild, dull but persistent headaches. He decided to confide in his curandeiro. He got there before dawn. After settling down to business, the curandeiro turned to Araujo.

"Are you under some kind of pressure?" the curandeiro asked.

"I'm just trying to come to terms with what I have gone through these last few months," Araujo said.

"Does that mean that you were under pressure?" the curandeiro asked again.

"Certainly, yes," he replied.

He told him the story of his wife's pregnancy and illness.

"Yes, I see," said the curandeiro. "But as a man, do you know what you should do?"

"Yes," he replied, "go back to the beginning, to the same bed and create another baby."

"You speak well. But tell me, is this, eh, scratching interfering with that process?" the medicine man enquired.

"Yes, there is a general lack of enthusiasm. I do not feel the urge and when I do feel the urge, the strength is not there," he said sadly.

"That's a complex one. Let's go over the chain of events again. Don't hurry. You have already paid for the consultation," the curandeiro coaxed Araujo.

Araujo related his story once more, concealing only the fact that he had consulted another curandeiro about six months before. That curandeiro had asked him whether he had been to the big city and he had denied it. In Culamawe, villagers were not quite comfortable with men or women who had been to the big city. There was talk of an incurable disease, which those people of the city were accused of spreading.

"I am not saying that there is no truth in what some reckless people are saying, but I would like to know whether you have been to the big city in the last several months!" the curandeiro asked Araujo.

"No. I have been very busy on my farm. In fact, I have not been there for a year," he replied.

"Good. It does not make my work easier, but it has cleared one potential obstacle," the curandeiro enlightened.

"And what is that?" Araujo asked.

"It is not for you to ask questions," the curandeiro said smugly.

"But this is important to me," Araujo insisted.

"Not if what you have told me is correct," the medicine man said with finality.

Araujo was quiet for a while, pensive. He remembered the day. He had been saving money in order to finance an all-expenses-paid trip to the city. He was the financier of the visit. He was his own benefactor.

The prime reason for the visit was to buy appropriate attire for his wedding.

After selecting and paying for a light-blue jacket, a white shirt, grey trousers and a decent pair of imported used shoes, he found himself with sufficient funds to finance an outing. He ended up drinking himself stupid, dancing like John Travolta and finally ending up in bed with a total stranger.

"Ah, yes," Araujo agreed. "I have been to the big city. I'm sorry to have lied. I did not think it was important.

"I should have thought so. Did you do what I suspect you did?" his curandeiro asked.

"What do you mean by that?" Araujo asked, confused.

"Did you use a condom?" the curandeiro clarified.

"Yes; no. I did not." Araujo responded.

"That also clears another obstacle," the curandeiro observed.

"I'm sorry I did not know," Araujo said apologetically.

"It is good that you should not know." The curandeiro said calmly. "This disease that they are talking of is being spread through the use of condoms. How many victims have come here confessing that they had been using condoms?"

"How very wicked of the manufacturers!" Araujo lashed out.

"For millions of years it was body to body, as ordained by God. And now…see what they have done to us. Listen to me young man. My father was a curandeiro. His father was a curandeiro and his grandfather had been a curandeiro before him. I know what I'm talking about. The wisdom of our ancestors protected us all these years, and it will protect us now. On your knees, young man, on your knees!" the curandeiro ordered.

Araujo went down on his knees.

"Shut your eyes, young man. Shut your eyes!" the curandeiro gave further instructions.

Araujo shut his eyes.

The curandeiro went into top gear. He cleared his throat and chanted:

> Protect him God of Monamatapa!
> Protect him God of Shaka!
> Protect him God of Kabaka!
> Protect him God of Makonde!
> Oh Yeka yeka, protect him!
> Oh Yeka yeka, protect him!
> Oh Yeka yeka, protect us!

After a long cleansing ceremony, Araujo was given his proscriptions and prescriptions, as well as a concoction to be used when taking a bath.

By the time they left each other, the curandeiro had told him a lot of mind-boggling stories. For example, the director whose car had rolled and overturned five times and yet the director was not even scratched.

"That was my toughest assignment. Just imagine a car overturning five times! In a normal accident no one would survive. I tell you it was a trying moment for me. But I succeeded! I did it!" he said triumphantly.

Araujo was amazed at the power of this curandeiro. He looked at him blankly like an empty calabash, waiting to be filled.

"Yes," the curandeiro continued, "I did it, but if I turn my wrath against you…that's another matter. Yes, that's another story. I can make you drown in a teacup, and mark my words! Even when I was young I made a man who had sneered at my bare feet walk around with a swollen toe for five years. He couldn't look at a shoe without being frightened. He had to come and kneel before me. I forgave him. Maybe you know him. He wears a big shoe and now works at the customs office."

"Your power is well-perceived," Araujo concurred.

"Not by all," he said as he bade Araujo farewell. "But let me not dwell on that. I will see you on the appointed day."

True, this was a serious curandeiro. You see, he was also credited with having stopped a young 'explorer' from going to America. The young 'explorer' had all the documents ready: the visa, the scholarship, the ticket, pocket money - everything. But the curandeiro had promised his client that the fellow was going nowhere.

So when the young 'explorer' died from 'a short illness bravely borne,' (according to the newspaper) just days before the scheduled departure, those in the know nodded in acknowledgement. He was indeed the alpha and omega, in many cases.

Araujo was therefore feeling confident of winning that battle against this so-called condom disease.

He remembered the curandeiro's question. If it is true that AIDS came from the green monkey and first appeared in Europe or America, who was doing what to who? Were they making love with green monkeys?

His belief was reinforced when three days later his wife returned to him. She confided in him that she had left against her mother's will. The mother would understand the actions of a dedicated young lover.

"My mother cannot give me a new baby. Why should I waste my time there?" she had told him.

After dinner Araujo had said to Maria: "Come, my only one. We have to sow the seeds while the garden is fertile."

They had retired to bed early, but his efforts were frustrated by fears from deep inside. Araujo lay awake in the arms of Maria and punished himself with scary thoughts.

"Don't worry about that Araujo," she told him. "I know your anxiety, but take your time. I am just happy to be with you. Try and sleep a little."

"But why, Maria, why? Why now? I have been waiting for you for so long!" he ranted.

"That is why you must take your time. The knot of time has to be untied. Just relax and time will reward you," she tried to comfort him.

Nevertheless, the realisation that her husband was less than strong on their first encounter since she returned from her mother made her feel less than secure.

'What has happened to my husband?' she found herself wondering. 'God knows I need a strong husband now. I cannot wait. I need a man as strong as a bull. That's what I need. But let me give him a chance first. No more than a chance! A young woman like me cannot claim to be married, and have nothing to show for it. There must be evidence that the marriage exists. There must be evidence of normality between us. There must be children,'

"Where? Where is my child? Where is…"

"Maria! Maria!" shouted Araujo. "Wake up, Maria. What is happening to you?"

Maria woke up from her reminiscing. "Nothing. What did you hear?" she asked.

"You were asking about the child! Are you all right, Maria?" her husband asked.

"Yes, I'm okay. Maybe just tired. It's a long journey, you know," she responded.

"You were shaking and sweating. I thought you were sick," he said.

"No dear. I'm fine." She assured him. "Let us try to sleep. We are both very tired."

****

Dona Rosa was in tears of joy the following day. She was so happy to see her daughter-in-law about the compound. Together they checked on the vegetable garden, the maize garden and the cassava garden near the stream. Maria told her all about the people at her mother's place and her stay there. They joked and laughed and joked some more. They made meals and ate together and talked endlessly.

"Maria, you have to listen to an old woman, every now and then, you know?" she said jokingly.

"And what does the old woman want to tell me?" Maria responded.

"When God closes one door, he opens another one, you know?" she asked a rhetorical question.

"I did not know you were that religious," Maria answered.

"Come, sit here and I will tell you," she said.

Maria sat beside her. "Don't bother telling a man about this. No man will ever understand. All he can do is get you pregnant with his baby, then wander around, waiting for his son or daughter, never knowing what's going on inside a woman." She paused for effect and also to take stock of the impression she was making on Maria. "His son or daughter is growing inside you and all he can do is wait around, play the fool or the angel who goes around dishing life."

"But that is how God made him!" Maria pointed out.

"Yes. That is why we must be in control. He thinks he is in charge but no, he isn't. It is for you to watch the stars, the moon and the sun. You decide when the time is right. Man cannot do that," she concluded.

"Yes, I guess the old woman is right," said Maria.

"You, of course, think that Araujo is my first child," she continued, gravely.

"What?" Maria asked in shock realisation.

"I don't blame you. Nobody here knows. I had the misfortune of losing my first baby, my only daughter," she sobbed.

Maria held her hand and caressed it.

"My late husband was then working in Quelimane. I had no relatives to turn to. It was a nightmare," she said amidst sobs.

"Oh, mother, don't cry," Maria said as she joined her in crying.

The two women sobbed for several minutes, each remembering a part of their lives, which they knew no man could understand, no matter how hard he tried.

"But, Maria, you know what made me strong?" Dona Rosa said, as she recovered from the trauma. "He held me in his arms and said 'I will give you another child, OK? Another child! A son!' That is what gave me comfort, the promise of a brighter future. That is why I told you God opens other doors," Dona Rosa reflected.

"I shall treasure your advice, mother," Maria promised.

"Remember, you have the key to his heart and to your happiness," Dona said. Then she rose and led the way back to the compound.

****

Araujo thought he was in excellent form and condition that evening. He could swear that the juices flowing within him matched those that great warriors were carved from. Was it not time that another great warrior rose from amongst his people? Was it ordained that a man, such as he was, could not be the path by which his great people rose again? No. He would rise to the occasion. He would straighten the main root as a good carver should, and strike the iron while it is still flaming hot.

Was it not said that on the night that Shaka the Zulu was conceived his father had eaten a lion's heart? Well, Araujo had just cleared a large portion of *massa* with a whole tiger fish and plenty of relish.

"That should do it," he muttered to himself.

---

massa - pap

"Maria!" he called out. "I need some water to wash my feet."

When Maria brought the water she asked him if he was not going to play draughts with the village men.

"No, Maria. Why should I spend time with them when I should be talking to my wife? You know them. They are a lousy lot. Just playing draughts and gossiping. I can no longer stand them."

"Oh, that's a major discovery. I was just going to sit and talk to the old lady," Maria countered.

"Not tonight. Tonight you talk to me," he said suggestively.

Dona Rosa was quite pleased with herself. She had done what many mothers-in-law found difficult to do. Instead of keeping aloof, she had engaged her daughter-in-law and the trick had worked. She had played the role of a leveller. She needed to keep this up and their relationship would blossom afresh and bring *camaraderie* and happiness into the family. She had been working from scratch, you see, because her own mother-in-law had died long before she got married to Eugenio. Her tenacity and patience were beginning to pay dividends. The only enemy that could interfere with that process would have to be a paid curandeiro. Who could possibly wish that they should not be a close-knit family? Her curandeiro would handle that, she reasoned. Her son and daughter-in-law had to have the best that this rural life could offer. That demanded the services of a curandeiro. First, she had to convince Maria and then Araujo would fall in place effortlessly. She would take her sweet time. But her sweet time boiled down to a few days.

****

Serious curandeiros do not sleep. They prowl the land by night. They visit their shrines by night. They lay traps and instal protective charms at night. They are nocturnal operators. The majority of their patients and clients have to book night appointments. That is also the time when the underworld moves. That is the time when ghosts and spirits take charge of rural paths, streams, caves and shadowy places. That is the time when shadows spring to life and spirits take human form and ghosts laugh at mortals.

That was the time when Benito entered the dimly-lit house of Curano Mbabane, a little known curandeiro, whose activities were conducted strictly through contacts. You could not reach him, unless introduced by a contact. Benito's contact was a man called Renalto Borges. He had cured Renalto of impotence and restored his virility in total, after a nasty accident had devastated his sexual life.

"I have come, as you know, to consult you on a number of issues," Benito intoned by way of introduction.

"A number of issues?" asked the curandeiro sharply.

"No, actually one issue," Benito said. "I need your protection."

"From what, young man, do you need protection?" enquired the curandeiro.

"Even from myself," replied Benito.

"I see you need total protection, from the known to the unknown," reflected Curano Mbabane.

"That is why I have come to you," Benito said calmly.

"You are a wise man, son of Vanga; a wise young man; perhaps a little too wise for your age, but that is beside the point. You have made the right decision at the right time. Let us examine the facts…"

Curano Mbabane spread a mat upon which he beckoned Benito to sit. Benito sat at one corner of the mat. The curandeiro spread his tools in the middle of the mat. He put his hands together and made several guttural noises whilst kneeling on one knee. Then he rose and spat in his hands and then rubbed them together until the spittle dried. Then he started pulling an invisible cord out of the air; he pulled and pulled until it appeared to have tightened around something slightly above his head. He tied an invisible knot in the air and slowly turned to Benito.

"Do you have a brother who is older than you?" he asked Benito.

"Yes, his name is…" Benito responded.

"Don't tell me what I have not asked," the curandeiro cut in. "Do you know where he is right now?"

"At home with his wife, I guess," Benito replied.

"Brilliant! Right now he is at home with his wife. Can you imagine what they are doing?" the curandeiro asked.

"No. I can't," replied Benito in muted anger.

"You can't imagine what your brother and his wife are doing at home at this hour? You can't imagine?" persisted the curandeiro.

"No, I can't. My mind is blank," replied Benito.

"You are sure about that?" insisted the curandeiro.

"Yes, I swear," said Benito.

"Swear by your forefathers!" ordered Curano Mbabane.

"I swear by them!" Benito hissed.

The curandeiro eyed him surreptitiously.

"You are a good man, son of Vanga," the curandeiro said. "It means you do not covet your brother's wife. It means you love your brother."

The curandeiro then looked at the invisible knot, ran his fiery eyes down until he was looking directly at Benito's eyes and said, "There is no danger from your brother. Tell me, son of Vanga. Do you have a younger brother?"

"No, I do not. I'm the last of only three brothers. There are no sisters," Benito volunteered before Curano Mbabane could stop him.

"And where is your other brother?" he asked.

"With his ancestors," replied Benito.

"We cannot deny our ancestors their rights, can we? Have any of your clansmen crossed your path?" Curano Mbabane continued to ask Benito.

"Not anyone that I know of," the son of Vanga responded.

"And have you crossed anybody's path?" the medicine man asked.

"I don't think so," Benito answered, "not deliberately, anyway."

"You would do well to keep off other people's affairs, especially their women," the curandeiro warned. "Do you suffer from any chronic disease?"

"No. Only coughs, colds and malaria," Benito responded.

"I'm talking of serious diseases like syphilis, diabetes, tuberculosis, epileptic fits or impotence. Do you suffer from any of them?" the curandeiro specified.

"Fortunately, no," Benito confirmed.

"Now tell me, son of Vanga, have you offended our ancestors by using contaminated rubber to protect yourself from our women?" Mbabane asked.

"I do not know whether they are contaminated or not, but I have not yet had reason to use them," observed Benito.

"Would I assert that they were contaminated if, indeed, they were wholesome?" Curano Mbabane asked lividly.

"I'm sorry if I implied that, sir," Benito said apologetically.

"Do you now find that you have any reason to use them in the near future?" the curandeiro asked.

"No, sir. I find no reason whatsoever to use them," responded Benito.

"Listen, son of Vanga. There is a danger that we must avoid; we who believe in the protection of our ancestors, we who exhort and seek that protection. The white man fought our ancestors. He sought to stymie our growth. He sought to keep our population down, so that he could claim that our land was bare and uninhabited and, therefore, available to his people. When our ancestors' resilience defeated the invaders' aims, the white man temporarily abandoned his quest to decimate our people. Now he is back amongst us. He is busy sowing diseases in our midst and claiming that a condom can save us! A condom developed by him, in secret, in his own land, whose ingredients nobody but he knows!"

He paused, but his eyes were piercing through Benito and seemingly through the wall, into the darkness outside.

Benito lowered his head and nodded, although he had not quite understood the import of Mbabane's accusation. If true, then the white man had a grand cruel design for the rest of the world, especially Africa. He could easily reduce the black population to a mere fraction of what it is today, within the next generation.

"Tell me son, of Vanga, do you know anybody who got this disease they are talking about without using a condom?"

"No, I do not," Benito, replied.

"It is a lie, Benito," said Curano Mbabane. "The white man first tried family planning but Africa was not ready for that. The man with the condom said we should plan our families using the condom. The man in the collar, the man of his God, said we should go out and multiply. I ask you son of Vanga, which of them was telling the truth?"

Benito had no answer. It was a debate he was ill-prepared for. But he knew that the Bible had commanded mankind to go out and multiply. The war had claimed hundreds of thousands of lives. It would be insensitive to tell the people not to multiply. The country did not have enough people. It needed manpower, and short of importing that manpower, the people had to procreate.

"That is our dilemma," said Curano Mbabane. "We do not have a ready answer."

He shook his head vigorously, shifted his position and again looked at Benito.

"Now then, let's look at the other side of the coin. This world is full of evil beings; evil people; even evil friends. It is this evil that you have to prepare for." He stood up and moved away from the mat. "On your belly young man, on your belly!" he ordered Benito.

The ritual took half an hour or so. Then Benito emerged from the hut with all defences in place. They included a bead lace to be worn on the left wrist all the time. He was back at home before the second cockcrow.

CHAPTER TWO

LOOSE NUTS

"You were up rather early, my son. What is troubling you?" Dona Rosa asked Benito in the morning.

"Oh, Mother, you don't ask a young man why he was up early. I just wanted to see the early morning stars," he replied jovially.

"Did you see them?" the mother persisted.

"Oh, yes. I saw the Morning Star, and then the first rays of the sun," he clarified evasively.

"They say that is the time when the ghosts return to the river," Dona Rosa said. "Do not stand in their way."

"Are you that superstitious?" Benito asked.

"It is the truth," his mother snapped.

"But how do you know it is the truth?" asked Benito.

"Your father told me," she replied with finality.

"Did he tell you what time they left the river?" Benito enquired.

"Nobody knows that," she said.

"But then how do they know that the ghosts return to the river? Didn't he tell you that?" Benito asked mockingly.

"They take their victims with them," Dona Rosa said sadly. "Did you know the son of Mourinho Borges?"

"Which one? Renalto? What about him?" asked Benito.

"He was last seen being led by a crocodile towards the bushy island in the middle of the Zambezi River. That was three days ago," she said tearfully.

"But I was with him... I ...I saw him four days ago!" Benito said, shaken.

"That was four days ago," she answered. "Four days is a long time, son."

Maria's warm and smooth hand touched his knee gently, and then went up slowly, caressing his inner thigh. Then she hesitated. The leg was shaking and rather cold. 'Very sensitive,' she thought. She felt her way further up. She had almost touched his manhood when Araujo's hand landed on hers.

"Don't do that. I'm not ready yet," he shouted.

She withdrew her hand and waited. After an eternity, she placed her hand on his chest. She stroked the nipples and held them between her fingers and gently rolled them one after the other. Then her hand moved over his tummy to the navel area and then onto the hairy patch below. Once again, his hand landed on hers.

"Can't you wait? I said wait a minute!" Araujo shouted.

She bit her lip. 'What the hell is going on here,' she wondered. 'You hold the key to his heart,' her mother-in-law had said. 'Control, Maria, control! You must be in control!'

She waited, her mind racing through recent events. He was so full of himself this evening. What went wrong? What's in his mind? Another woman? Other women? If it were other women, would he have insisted on going to bed so early? What is troubling him?

Then he stirred. He was now on his knees. His hand touched her waist-beads band.

"Move a bit. This way. I mean down. Come down a bit."

She moved as requested. Her heart thumped, expectantly.

"There, not that way. Up a bit. Further. There," he murmured impatiently. "Don't touch it. I said don't! Don't move! Fuck it! You've spoilt everything!" Araujo shouted even louder.

"But I'm trying to be of help," Maria said softly.

"What help? You call this help? What's wrong with you, Maria? You were not like this…" he snapped.

"I'm sorry," she whimpered.

"You might as well be! God Almighty!" he was livid.

Maria sat in bed and sobbed weakly, while Araujo pretended to be asleep. They were so close and yet so far apart. Araujo had blamed Maria for his failure and yet he knew Maria was innocent. That goaded him all the more because he knew she was actually trying to be helpful. But, why would a 'normal' man be in need of help to make love to his wife? He loved her and she loved him. That is all that counted. What other help did he need? Had he not eaten pap with tiger fish? Maybe it was too soon after the meal.

Maria thought she understood. Yet his failure to rise to the occasion troubled her. He had to blame her. That was natural. The devil is always the other guy! But why did he say that she had changed? Was she not the same old Maria that he had married just over a year earlier? No, there must be somebody else in his life. She shouldn't have gone to her mother for so long, she regretted.

* * * * * * * * * *

After a late breakfast, Araujo and Benito walked out of the compound together. Dona Rosa and Maria watched them turn left at the gate and disappear up the path.

They had put out a sack outside Dona Rosa's house and were busy spreading shelled maize to dry. Dona Rosa intended to take the maize to the grinding mill, which an aid agency had bought for the community, a large number of whom were returnees from Malawi. The aid agency was helping to re-settle some of the war-displaced people in Culamawe. The school, the water-pump and the grinding mill were key developments in this process.

"Did they say they would be back in time for lunch?" Maria asked Dona Rosa.

"I forgot to ask them, but I'm sure they will," replied Dona Rosa.

"What shall we prepare for lunch?" Maria wondered.

"Come, let us check in the garden," Dona Rosa suggested.

"You are always consulting the garden for answers," observed Maria.

"Yes, a farmer talks to her garden and the garden brings forth all its fruits and grains and tubers. It has the answers that I need," she lectured.

The two women went off to the garden. The cassava and arrowroots were waiting for them. Just dig up and there's food for you!

"Did you have a good night's rest?" asked Dona Rosa, not without a pinch of excitement.

"Yes," Maria answered quickly.

"By which you mean all went according to plan?" asked Dona Rosa.

"Not exactly, but…" Maria said reluctantly.

"Yes?" she waited anxiously.

"I can't explain. Maybe another day," Maria tried to sound convincing.

"Right. You cannot till the garden and plant on the same day," her mother-in-law said.

"I guess you are right, Mother," responded Maria.

"Tonight we'll have arrowroots and cassava," she added.

****

"How is your new girlfriend?" Araujo asked his brother. They were crossing the stream that separated their farm from that of the nearest neighbour.

"I do not have a girlfriend," Benito replied.

"Yes, you have. You think everybody is blind?" Araujo continued. "Why haven't you brought her home?"

"All right, she is not my new girlfriend. She is just a friend," Benito replied, unconvincingly.

"She seems to be taking quite a bit of your time," Araujo persisted. "Any serious intentions, or are you searching for fleeting moments of romanticism?"

"I'm still thinking about it." After a moment's silence, Benito said, "Do you think it's a good idea?"

"The thinking or the bringing her home?" Araujo asked rhetorically.

"OK. I see your point," Benito said.

"So, when is she coming home?" Araujo seemed to be in a hurry to meet her.

"You'll be the first to know, old boy. Just let me think about it," Benito promised without definite commitment. They walked on silently for a while. Then Benito turned to his brother. "And you, how are you getting on... with Maria?"

Araujo did not reply immediately. His mind shot back to the previous night and his inadequacies. He had wanted to discuss the matter with his brother, man to man and, hopefully, get this heaviness off his chest. After all, this was his brother, his only brother and the only real friend he knew.

"There is a problem," he started and then shut up.

"A problem?" enquired Benito. "Tell me about it."

"This is strictly between you and me," he began.

"You can count on me," Benito assured him. "Any help you might need do not hesitate to ask me."

"You see, when she came back from hospital and her mother's place, I was not sure whether I wanted to or whether she wanted to… you know? I wasn't sure how to proceed." He paused.

"Quite naturally, you needed to take time," Benito tried to fill the vacuum.

"Right, her very words! In so doing I let her down. But she took it like a mature woman. Last night it happened again. I do not know what to say," Araujo revealed.

By this time they had reached the canteen. Benito bought two beers and the two brothers sat under a tree shade and talked, away from the rest of the patrons.

"I know the problem has to do with me," Araujo continued, "I can feel it."

"Have you seen anybody about it?" Benito asked.

"Naturally," Araujo responded.

"And what did he say?" asked Benito.

"Just took my money and told me stories confirming his real and perceived powers. I'm beginning to doubt these curandeiros!" Araujo railed.

"Are you suggesting that the whole exercise was fruitless?" enquired Benito.

"No. Not at all. All I'm saying is that I do not know how far to trust them," Araujo said.

"Whom did you see?" Benito asked curiously.

"Antonio Phiri. He spent a lot of time in Malawi during the early years of the civil war," Araujo explained. "He is well-known. But I think he overplays his competence, especially in the area of this new disease."

"You mean HIV/AIDS?" Benito asked.

"Yes. It has made him very popular," responded Araujo.

"His discovery that AIDS is transmitted through the use of condoms is explosive. But don't you think it makes sense? I mean all these thousands of years without AIDS and without condoms, and then bang! The condoms come and AIDS follows! What do you make of it?" Araujo watched his brother as he tried to find suitable words to respond.

"Of course, he is right," Benito finally said. "I hear that they have even allowed him to advertise his services on the radio. That will make him unreachable! Imagine the queues!"

"I don't know whether to go back to him or find another," Araujo admitted his ambivalence.

"I think you should talk to him first. If things do not improve, we can always think of someone else," Benito advised. "Does Maria know of the earlier visit?"

"No way! I can't involve her in these matters," Araujo enlightened.

"But tell me frankly. Have you ever used a condom?" Benito asked.

"Never, and I don't intend to," answered Araujo.

"Me too, Never will," concurred Benito.

They remained quiet for a minute. Benito had other thoughts.

"Do you mind if I don't come home for lunch?" Benito asked his brother. "I have to see her."

"Is she that irresistible?" Araujo asked light-heartedly.

"I can resist anything …but temptation," Benito said.

"You got that from her?" Araujo asked.

"I told you she is a genius," Benito said boastfully.

"Where should I say you have gone?" asked Araujo.

This prompted Benito to tell his brother a joke. A lawyer had asked a witness where he lived.

"I live with my brother," answered the witness.

"Very well," said the lawyer. "And where does your brother live?"

"He lives with me."

"Alright, and where do both of you live?"

"We live together."

"Maybe you should rephrase the question," interrupted the judge.

****

The arrowroots and the cassava did not help much. On the contrary, Araujo suspected that they were the cause of his quite unexpected coughing fits. In his view, it couldn't have been the beer, because he only drank two and that was much earlier in the day. It was definitely the evening meal that had provoked the coughing, he concluded.

"How did you cook the damn cassava?" he asked his wife, between bouts of coughing.

"In the normal way," replied Maria.

"And you call this the normal effect, I suppose?" he asked sarcastically.

"Who would have expected that kind of reaction?" she challenged.

"Couldn't you think of any other dish?" he asked.

"It was Mother's suggestion," she defended.

"So now you want to blame my mother, do you?" he sneered.

"No, I'm only saying that she suggested the dish for the evening meal," she said. "It was only natural because we were in the cassava garden.

"Well, you can tell her I enjoyed the stuff very much," he said angrily.

That sealed her hopes for that night. He did not even face her. He coughed and cursed several times. Then he fell asleep. Maria was angry; but she did not allow it to show, neither in her voice nor in her manner. She bottled it up somewhere and resolved to have a frank talk with Araujo's mother the following day. Her husband, Araujo, was behaving strangely, quite apart from the bouts of coughing. His inability to communicate with her, as his wife, as a man should, disturbed her. His inadequacies or, better still, his refusal to perform his marital duties and his inexplicable attitude towards her goaded her. She had to discuss all that with his mother. She had suffered enough. Things had to change. Or else?

His mother had said that God opened other doors? He would have to open other doors for her. Araujo had not been cruel to her, as cruel generally went. But was this not cruelty, this denial of her right to marital bliss? She knew Culamawe was a gender-unequal society like the rest of Africa. She had seen it, experienced it through her friends, and now she was living it.

This was a society where women played second fiddle. One of her friends, Joana Rebello, was ejected from her house because she had dared to ask her husband to use a condom. How many women in her society could even dream of asking, let alone persuading, their husbands to stick to protected sex?

The following morning, even the sun rose reluctantly. It looked as if it wanted to go back to its bed of golden rays on the eastern horizon.

The birds chirped without the usual enthusiasm and the usually loud croaking of frogs was a distant occasional sound. Dona Rosa's cocks had not crowed that morning. Or maybe Maria had somehow failed to hear them. This was by no means a normal day!

Dona Rosa's hut was a respectable distance away from that of her son, Araujo. But that did not provide soundproofing against the altercation between her son and daughter-in-law. She had clearly heard some nasty exchange of words or, to put it more accurately, her son's curses and accusations. At one time, she had felt like opening her door and confronting them.

But reason had prevailed and she had lain on her bed with her fingers in her ears, putting a lid on an explosive situation. But her curiosity was so intense that she had to listen. So she uncorked her ears and strained to catch every word that was uttered. She only dozed off when it became clear that sleep had overtaken Araujo; but not before she had resolved to talk to him and her daughter-in-law the following morning. But talk about what?

She couldn't discuss the intimate details of their relationship. That was out of bounds. She couldn't say that she had heard the whole story. In fact, she had not. She had heard her son's loud charges and curses, but she had not heard Maria's responses, if any.

That being so she had to tread very carefully like a heavyweight crossing marshy ground. Moreover, she had a duty to keep them together as far as possible. She couldn't imagine a serious rift between them. It would lead to separation and divorce and acrimony and vengeance or, worse still, a vendetta. She dreaded vendettas. A family pitted against itself is no family. It would eventually be brought down on its knees. In this region when a family takes on another family, it is total war, no half-measures. It is a battle to the last man and, oftentimes, to the last woman! The adversaries use any and all means at their disposal. They kill, maim and kill. They take no prisoners of war. It is a dastardly bloody war!

The winners are only the curandeiros. They advise on how to win the battle, not on how to win the war. Battles are to be won, not lost. Wars are to be stopped, not won. The curandeiros cannot stop the war, but they can win you battles at a handsome price. Dona Rosa wanted to win the battle and stop the war. It was a tall order, but Dona Rosa was an energetic, resourceful woman.

Maria had second thoughts. If she presented herself before her mother-in-law before Araujo woke up, he would conclude that she had gone to campaign against him. If she left it until he woke up, he might pretend that there was nothing wrong and blame her if she raised the issue later. What was she to do? How was she to scale this risky marital ladder? How was she to dive into the pool without causing any ripples?

But remember, if you go to battle with an assault rifle, you cannot pretend that all you have is a kitchen knife. She had the assault rifle, and God knows what Araujo had in his armoury.

She opened her eyes and looked at the ceiling. The light was filtering into the room via the normal spaces in an African grass-thatched house. Africans are claustrophobic by nature and the open spaces are their natural link to the outside world. She needed to go out there and present her grievances to the mother of her husband. She began to get out of bed.

"Where are you going?" shouted Araujo, who apparently was very much awake.

"Nowhere, in particular," she replied. "It is daylight. I want to get up."

"I need some soup; chicken soup," he ordered.

That is all that Maria needed, an excuse to get out and talk to his mother. Whether by design or unwittingly he had given her the opportunity that she had been looking for, to talk to her mother-in-law. She wrapped a loose garment over her nightdress and got out. She called out only once.

"Come in, I'm awake," Dona Rosa answered.

"It is Araujo, he needs chicken soup," Maria explained.

"Is he all right?" Dona Rosa asked.

"He coughed too much last night," Maria revealed.

"What's the problem?" Dona Rosa asked, as she got out of bed.

"I do not know. We need to talk," replied Maria.

Dona Rosa's chickens were alarmed, as usual, when she grabbed one of their rowdy cocks and headed for the water-point, that is, the only tap where the family drew water. They knew that the cock would not return to them alive.

In the meantime, Maria had kindled the fire and balanced on the stove a kettle full of water. If the cock's memory were not so short, it would have remembered the purpose of that water.

As soon as the water came to the boil, Dona Rosa got hold of the cock, twisted its head, placed it on a stone and with a sharp knife cut the throat, leaving only a piece of flesh holding together the head and the rest of the body. The cock had no chance against Dona Rosa's powerful hands and determination. A cock had to die to solve her son's coughing problems! The pot with the boiling water took over. The dead cock was immersed in it and a few minutes later, the feathers were coming off at the slightest pull. Less than one hour later both soup and meat were ready for Araujo. That was Araujo's chicken! The other peripheral consumers did not count. Araujo was the main consumer. He was the reason for the cock's exit. In Africa, cocks are not just eaten; they are eaten for a cause.

Maria remembered the story of the proud cock and the fattened ram. The cock hated the ram so much that it made a point of standing on the roof of its master's house three times a day and crowing loudly to the effect that a visitor should come so that the ram may be eaten. When eventually a visitor appeared, the master decided that the visitor was not senior enough to warrant the slaughter of a whole fattened ram. A cock would do, he told his wife. The ram smiled at the cock and said simply, "Pride comes before..."

As the two women watched Araujo consume his portion of the chicken and soup, there was an upsurge of enthusiasm for solidarity, for standing together on the face of sinister forces. It was not the time to bring up issues that were bound to cause friction and discord. The two women silently resolved not to trouble Araujo with the events of the previous night. None knew what the other was thinking but empathy can, at times, be contagious. They retracted their claws and the day passed uneventfully.

But the coughing returned at night with renewed tenacity. Even Araujo had to admit that he was now feeling progressively weaker. He now knew it had nothing to do with the cassava and arrowroots. What was it? 'Flu? Malaria? Did Maria have any medicine with her? He decided to ask.

"Yes," she said. "I have one or two aspirins." She fetched them and he took the two tablets.

"Not good for malaria but flu might respond," he said, after swallowing them.

Half an hour later, the coughing eased somewhat and he was able to sleep. But for how long? He was up by midnight, and again at about four in the morning, with dry coughs that sapped strength and confidence.

By morning, even Dona Rosa had decided that the matter needed her direct intervention. She could not just sit there and watch her son wither. Her daughter-in-law was of a similar view. Maria wanted to help her husband. It was her duty to preserve his health. That was one viewpoint that both Dona Rosa and Maria shared. So what was the problem?

"I see no problem at all about going to a curandeiro," Dona Rosa asserted, with her eyes fixed on Maria. "We have to find out the cause or causes of his problem. That is what we must do, Maria."

"Why not take him to hospital first, and then, depending on the outcome, try the other," Maria suggested.

"No, it's a waste of money. The curandeiro will treat him and, at the same time, tell us what the problem is. He is my son; he will do what I want him to do!"

"But he is my husband!" Maria shouted.

"It is not the same thing!" Dona Rosa said curtly.

"What are you insinuating by that?" Maria asked.

"Nothing. You don't know what my son needs," Dona Rosa continued. "He is your husband but you don't know what is good for him. Not yet."

"If you cared one moment about him, you would take him to hospital first," Maria said accusingly.

"Yes, I care," Dona Rosa shouted. "I have cared since before he was born. I have cared all those years. Don't accuse me of not caring, young woman. What do you know about caring?"

At that very moment, Araujo managed to step out of the house. "What's the matter with you two?" he asked gravely.

"Ask her," Maria answered.

"No, ask her," Dona Rosa shouted.

"I'm asking both of you," Araujo insisted.

"I'm simply telling her that we have to see a medicine man to ascertain the cause of these problems and she just will not listen," Dona Rosa explained.

"She accused me of not knowing what is good for you," Maria answered.

"Now shut up both of you. Don't I have a role in this matter? Is it only what you want and not what I want for myself? I'm not going anywhere, if that's what you wanted to know."

He walked slowly to the latrine and helped himself and then returned and went back inside.

****

Benito's head was made of lead. If not, then it must have been made of a metal closely related to lead in weight. Otherwise it wouldn't be so heavy. Or, maybe it was the pillow that had a head-magnet. He couldn't decide. What was certain was that his head did not want to get up from the pillow that morning. His girlfriend had somehow managed to pull out of bed and was preparing breakfast.

"Lie still," she told him. "I'll prepare something to kill the hangover. How many times do I have to tell you to stop drinking Manica?"

"What else can one drink here?" he murmured.

"Drink water, for God's sake!" she argued.

"Man can't live on water alone," he assured her. "Have you forgotten what Jesus did? He turned water into wine and a dull party into a vibrant one."

"Your people must be wondering where you have disappeared to. Do they know you are here?" she asked matter-of-factly, trying to change the subject.

"My brother knows I'm with the most beautiful woman in Mozambique. Any other questions?" Benito asked.

She thought for a moment and then said lightly, "If you stopped flattering me, I might learn to like you a little bit."

"No apologies. I mean it. My only enemy right now is this stupid headache," he lamented. "Linda, please get me a beer. They say a beer in the morning kills the hangover fast. I should try that now."

"If you want to turn yourself into an alcoholic, that is," she concluded for him.

"Impossible! One beer can't turn even a rabbit into anything of the sort. If anything, it will give me another reason to drag you back into bed," he smirked.

Benito thought the conversation had cleared his head somewhat. He tried to turn his head. It was throbbing with pain.

"Enough bed games. We have to face the day," Linda said with finality.

Emilinda da Vila (affectionately known as Linda) hailed from Tete town. Her father had died during the civil war and her mother was a kiosk operator in the central market. Linda was the eldest of three children, two girls and a boy. She had studied hard in tough circumstances. When relative peace returned to the country, she was recruited as a primary school teacher and posted to the remote village of Culamawe. She protested but the authorities needed the teachers in those remote places. They told her to apply for transfer after two years, if she still felt uncomfortable.

They had met quite by chance. He had been returning home from visiting a distant relative in Tete to find out whether there was any possibility of employment of any kind there for him. Linda had entered the same bus, actually a lorry converted into a bus by the addition of a canvas roof and fixed benches to sit on, and sat next to the only decent-looking young man around. As it happened, she was going to Culamawe, and Benito was quick to offer to show her the school. She was grateful and happy to make her first acquaintance with a native of Culamawe. Friendship had developed quite rapidly and now, several months later, Benito found himself drawn closer and closer to Linda and her to him. There were three other teachers in the school but they were married and much older than Linda. She felt comfortable in the company of Benito Fato Vanga, the youthful, handsome son of Dona Rosa.

That morning she prepared something they called PTO, that is potato, tomato and onion soup, and cleared Benito's hangover pretty fast, but a slight headache persisted. Facing the day meant cleaning up, washing clothes and going to the market. But Benito had other ideas.

"If you would come in here a minute I promise to clean up and wash the clothes while you go to the market," he pleaded with Linda.

"First you clean up and wash the clothes, and then I'll come in there," she responded equally pleadingly.

After a short while, Benito emerged from the bedroom with some clothes to wash.

"That's more like it," said Linda. "I've got some more somewhere."

"You want to kill me with washing?" he complained.

"I'm sorry. I thought you were a strong man," she teased him.

"I am, but this is something else!" he said.

"All right lazy bones; I'll help you to iron them," she said sweetly.

Benito grunted and went over to the water-point at the back of the house. To keep his mind busy, while his hands washed the clothes, he tried to remember the best moments spent with her. Then a joke interrupted his thoughts.

Two soldiers had, just before going on a campaign, promised to help each other in case of need. While fighting, a grenade severed the leg of one of them. The comrade quickly put the injured soldier on his back and hurried towards the doctor's shelter. On the way, another grenade caught the head and severed it. The agitated soldier did not notice.

"Where are you going?" asked the platoon leader.

"I'm taking my injured comrade to the doctor," answered the soldier.

"Doctor? Whatever for? Can't you see he has no head?"

Shocked, the soldier dropped the body roughly onto the ground and on checking fumed,

"What a liar...this! He told me he had lost a leg when, in fact, it was the head!"

Benito wanted to relate the same to Linda but remembered that her father had died in the war. He turned to the clothes and rinsed furiously.

They spent the day together oblivious of the storm that was gathering in Dona Rosa's home.

CHAPTER THREE

KNOTS

Dona Rosa wasted no time. She had noticed something in Araujo's voice that said that all was not well. Her son was sick. Her other son was away without proper explanation and her daughter-in-law was behaving like a dunderhead.

"You go in there and tell him to come out," she told Maria. "He's got to take a bath and be ready to travel."

"You go and tell him," Maria responded impudently.

"Did you not say you are his wife?" she asked.

"Yes. And you said that you were his mother," she responded, annoyed.

"Then go and tell him to come out!" her mother-in-law ordered.

"I won't! You heard him say he isn't going anywhere. We have to respect his wishes," Maria said.

"Indeed. Even if he wishes to die, we should sit out here and respect his wishes! Is that what you call knowing what is good for him? Oh, no. That is the way to kill him! Is that what you want? Tell me, Maria, is that what you really want?" Dona Rosa asked bitterly.

Maria kept silent. What she really wanted was to get out of the place for good. Araujo was a sick man. He was in the grip of his mother who, no doubt, had absolutely no respect for her or her marriage to Araujo. The worst of it all was that she knew Araujo would not give her what she wanted. He was incapable of it and he knew it. That is what made him such a wreck.

"If you think I want to kill your son, you are wrong. But to put your mind at peace I'll go my way," she said, as tears welled up in her eyes.

Maria was a woman. Tears came easily to her eyes. But she had made up her mind. And once her mind was set, that was it. No change, no retreat. She had to liberate her mind; liberate her soul and liberate her person.

She had loved Araujo, maybe still loved him. But she knew he no longer could love her; not in the way he would have liked; and certainly not in the

36

way that would have made her happy. Ever since her return to him, he had acted hastily, erratically and insensitively. That was a serious flaw in his character. Had it been there all along? Had she also been insensitive at the beginning? Or what was it? Infatuation? She tried to remember when he last made love to her. When was it? Why was it not coming forward in her memory? It was all so vague, like a dream, like he had never really done it. But the first time! That was simply explosive. That she remembered very well. Hot, torrid and explosive. That is what she had loved, the passion. Could passion last? Does it last?

Maria did not have a great deal to pack. The feeble protests of Araujo notwithstanding, she got all her things together and left.

"I know you will come back to me," Araujo dreamt loudly.

"Maybe in the next life," replied Maria.

"Then, I might not be in need of you," he responded.

She left; frustrated but not bitter, not wanted, not liked and certainly not loved. Hard to believe?

Dona Rosa was standing outside her house watching as Maria emerged from Araujo's house. Maria glanced at her and stopped.

"He is all yours now," she said seriously. "Sometimes it is good to listen to what young people have to say, don't you think, Dona Rosa?"

Before the older woman could respond, Maria took her the bags and hurried out of the gate.

"You will regret that one day, Maria," Dona Rosa murmured to herself.

Maria had had her little revenge.

****

Benito went home on Sunday. Both his mother and his brother had been waiting for him anxiously.

Dona Rosa wanted him to help her in persuading Araujo to go to a curandeiro of her choice.

Araujo wanted him to accompany him to see Antonio Phiri, he of the Malawi fame.

"I'm glad you have come, Benito," Dona Rosa began without ceremony. "You can't imagine what I have gone through these last few days."

"What's the matter, Mother? Is Maria sick again?" Benito asked.

"That's another matter!" she answered.

"So what is it then?" Benito queried rapidly.

"It's your brother. He's unwell. We have to see somebody," Dona Rosa informed her son.

"Where is he?" Benito asked.

"He's in bed. Go talk to him," Dona Rosa advised.

"And Maria, where's she?" Benito asked.

"She's gone," his mother said.

"What do you mean, gone? Gone where?" Benito asked, puzzled.

"Where she belongs," Dona Rosa responded bluntly.

"They haven't quarrelled, have they?" he enquired.

"It's worse than that. He will tell you," his mother said.

Benito knocked at his brother's open door.

"Come in. Where have you been?" Araujo asked weakly.

"Just tell me how you are. What happened? When did this happen? Where is Maria? Oh, look at you. I shouldn't have left you alone!" Benito gasped.

Benito studied his brother's condition. "I'm not feeling that bad actually. But how do I look?" he asked Benito.

"Not as well as I expected. What happened? Can you sit up?" Benito asked.

Araujo sat in bed. He had lost some weight, but his unkempt hair made him look much worse. The coughing was deep and hollow, but unaccompanied by any significant release of sputum. As expected in such a situation, his eyes were red, dilated and sunken. He related the events of the last three days to Benito, who listened attentively like a consultant physician.

"Are you sure it's not malaria?" his brother asked.

"I'm not sure, but it's highly unlikely," Araujo enlightened.

"Did you take any medicines?" Benito continued asking.

"Yes, mother prepared the traditional anti-malaria stuff and I took it. I also took two aspirins from Maria. I can't say they haven't helped. But the cough is something else…" He broke into a spirited cough that seemed to take away all the air in his chest, leaving him gasping for oxygen. "Mother wants me to visit a medicine man of her choice. I would like to see my own man. What do you say?"

"As you please. You know my views from our chat the other day. When can we go? You shouldn't waste another day here!" Benito advised.

And so Dona Rosa was overruled. But she was at least relieved that he had agreed to consult a curandeiro instead of going to hospital. His choice of curandeiro had to be respected, although that did not mean that she would not have to consult her own curandeiro.

To begin with, she had total confidence in her own curandeiro. Besides, the curandeiro had advised against consulting other curandeiros before giving him what businessmen call 'the right of first refusal.' In other words, it was necessary to present the case to him first and, then, if need be, move on to another. That rule applied to her, not to Araujo, since he had never consulted her curandeiro.

The next day, two delegations left Dona Rosa's home in two different directions. They sought to find a cure for Araujo's illness and protection against recurrence. The first one to leave consisted of her two sons, the two brothers, Araujo and Benito. They headed north or, to be precise, north of northeast, where several hours later they hoped to arrive at the modest home of Antonio Phiri, curandeiro extraordinaire!

The other delegation, comprising solely of Dona Rosa, headed west, to the home of her curandeiro who, all things being equal, should be able to locate the problem assailing Araujo and arrest it or, to use Benito's expression, stop it in its tracks.

The second delegation knew about the first delegation but, as you have already guessed, the first had no idea about Dona Rosa's Plan B, as she called it. Why would a woman of her calibre and experience rely only on her son's choice of curandeiro? Were they not her sons?

How would they know about these matters better than her, a woman who had been consulting them since they were mere kids?

"Let them go. And for their sakes, I commend them to my very own protector, to deliver them hence and back, safely," Dona Rosa prayed.

Araujo and Benito had left at around five in the morning.

Dona Rosa started off after her prayers of commendation. The sun was late for the time of the year, but that was something to be grateful for. She did not want to meet other early birds. By the time the sun rose, the Vanga family home was deserted.

"What is she like?" Araujo asked Benito.

"You won't believe this," he answered. "That woman is an angel. She lives for me. I wish you were better; I would take you there. But she has agreed to come home during the school holidays. She is a darling, I tell you."

"Are you sure those teachers are not meddling with her when you are not there?" Araujo enquired.

"She won't let them. They respect her a lot," Benito sounded confident. "She has lots of books and we read quite a bit. I'm beginning to feel like a student in love with what he is studying. You know what joke she had for me the other day? A nephew wrote to his uncle demanding some pocket money. 'If you don't send me the money right away, I will blow out my brains with a revolver.' You know what the uncle replied? He said, 'this is the second time you have written threatening to do the same thing. I sent you a revolver and you pawned it. I am not going to fall into that trap again.'"

They laughed heartily as Benito searched for another joke to keep his brother's spirits up.

"Did I tell you the one about USA?" he asked Araujo.

"I can't remember; you have told me so many!" Araujo answered.

"Well, it's a short one. It's about the forester, you know, Carlos d'Ouro. He studied forestry in Cuba. When he came back he had lots of stories to tell. One fellow asked him whether he had been to USA.

"Almost, almost," replied Carlos.

"How can that be, almost, almost?"

"It can be, yes. I have been to Cuba and …the USA is just opposite."

After another bout of laughter, Araujo slowed down and stopped. Benito thought Araujo wanted to relieve himself, but that was not the case.

"Are you all right?" Benito asked him.

"Yes, just a little tired. These legs have not moved for three days. They need a little warming up," Araujo said.

They resumed walking after a short rest.

"I wonder why Mother was so rough with Maria?" Araujo said, seemingly out of the blue.

"Was she? What about?" Benito asked, curiosity gripping him. "I just thought she was. What would you have done?"

"Don't forget, women can be very rough sometimes, especially to each other," Benito offered. "There must be something that was said, something sensitive. I wonder what it was!" Araujo said, "Tell me, would Linda be upset if I told her that she did not know what is good for you?" he finally asked.

"She would be devastated. Is that what Maria said to Mother? That was callous of her," he said without waiting for Araujo's answer.

"No; it was Mother's challenge. Anyway, that's over now, water under the bridge," Araujo reflected as he trudged on.

"When I last visited Tete, I witnessed a very nasty incident." Benito recounted the episode animatedly. Two women in their late twenties were fighting tooth and nail, quite literally. After scratching and bloodying each other on the face and neck, they tore apart each other's clothes and then rolled over each other, biting the teats and any other vulnerable areas. "You would have thought they were cats," Benito concluded.

"It would have come to that if I had not intervened," Araujo observed.

"Do you think she will come back?" asked Benito. "I rather suspect so, myself."

"Leave that for Antonio Phiri." Araujo answered.

Dona Rosa was lucky. Her curandeiro was just returning home from a trip when she arrived. He was not expected that day. As such, there were no other clients waiting.

"Enough!" commanded the curandeiro after hearing her long story. "It is true we all love our children. But we cannot be their guardians forever. We can offer protection, within reason. But it is forbidden us to think that we will be there for them all the time. Did you give Maria extra advice on how to handle him when they are together?"

"Not quite like that, but…" she said.

"I see… not quite like that," he repeated.

"I just gave her a few words of wisdom," Dona Rosa continued, "just as a good mother-in-law should."

"I'm sure you did. Did you tell her she held the key to his heart?" he asked, suddenly baring his teeth, his wrinkles severe.

"I'm sure I did," she answered.

"Did she follow your advice?" he continued to ask.

"That is what I can't trust, not totally," she responded.

"The little bitch!" said the curandeiro. "Would you know if she gave him anything, anything at all, when he returned?" he asked.

"Like what?" she asked.

"I mean medicine for his illness," he said.

"Oh, yes. On the night he started coughing, she gave him some tablets. She said they were aspirins and also said something about lemon," Dona Rosa recalled.

"What was the reaction like, did he tell you?" he investigated.

"For a while, all was tranquil. Then, things became progressively capricious," she revealed.

"Did you see them, the tablets?" he asked.

"No," she answered.

"Did she administer any more drugs?" he enquired.

"Not as far as I know. She said they were all she had," she said.

"The bitch!" he yelled again. "I'm afraid to say she was on a mission. She gave the man a love potion disguised as medicine. You might call it a love potion or medicine for love. But she also wanted to control his libido. Instead, she inhibited its manifestation. Ah, women from the south! We must cut that umbilical cord! We must liberate the man. We must replenish his control. But, listen. She will not rest. She has locked horns with you. We can't let her win!"

"No, we can't!" Dona Rosa chanted.

"We must cut the link!" the curandeiro said.

"Yes, we must!" she agreed.

The curandeiro turned to a tiny cinder box containing some of the tools of his trade. He took out a razor blade.

"Give me your left hand," he commanded Dona Rosa who promptly obeyed. He got hold of the arm and examined it. There were two very faint marks made by a sharp object just above the wrist. These were incisions previously made by a curandeiro. He traced with his finger up the arm up to the elbow. Then he selected a spot where he planned to make a special incision in which to insert the protective drug. The drug itself was in a small bamboo pouch capped by a lid made of a hare's skin. He put the razor blade to use and quickly made three neat incisions. He put the powdery drug in the incisions and the blood, which was beginning to flow, clotted rapidly.

"She cannot harm you now, nor can she harm your son. She can only harm herself," he assured Dona Rosa in a shaky, hoarse voice. "We are watching her movements. We are firmly in control!"

In her time, Dona Rosa had seen many interesting incidents. On one occasion, a crocodile had been seen a long way from home. It was a kilometre from the nearest collection of water or river. It appeared to be determined to visit the home of Magaia Magaia, a charcoal dealer providing alternative energy to Canoa Village. The first villager to see it raised alarm and, shortly afterwards, some villagers converged near the scene.

"Let's kill it right away," volunteered one of them.

"No. This crocodile is no ordinary crocodile," replied another. "It appears to have been sent."

"But how could it have covered the distance between here and the river?" replied another.

"Search me!" a villager said.

"Search me!" replied another villager.

"In my opinion," said an obscure man with an equally obscure voice, "it must have covered three quarters of the journey in the form of a man and changed to a crocodile a few metres away from Magaia Magaia's home."

"That is the only plausible explanation," confirmed another knowledgeable villager.

"We, therefore, cannot interfere," concluded the obscure man.

That night, Magaia Magaia's ten-year-old daughter disappeared without trace.

She knew of another woman whose son had married a girl that the woman disliked intently. She had severally warned her son that it was unwise of him to even dream of marrying her. But the young man was in love and love couldn't be stopped. Alas! He was wrong. The woman consulted a very powerful curandeiro and, ten years later, the two lovers were still far from getting a child despite confirmation by medical doctors that both of them were clinically fertile and sexually active.

Then there was the case of the creditor who was chased by bees from the debtor's compound and stung to death. The bees had been sent by an awesome curandeiro.

Not to mention the tycoon who took Angonia by storm. He had gone there with a large briefcase full of new, high-denomination bank notes and bought a large ranch. Then he went to a stock-keeper whose cattle were apparently not doing very well because of the prevalence of tsetse flies, and bought all the cattle with liquid cash. Using a portion of the largess, the cattle seller consulted a very senior curandeiro.

"First, I want you to take the money," he said to Careca, the curandeiro, "then we can talk. I know I should have come to you a long time ago, when I bought my cows. But that's behind us now."

He counted a large batch of banknotes and proffered the money to the curandeiro.

"You know this is quite out of the ordinary," Careca observed, his mouth watering a little.

"But then my request is not ordinary either," replied the cattleman. "I have sold all my cattle to this man."

"Which man are you referring to?" Careca asked.

"This tycoon, you know, João Mali Mingi," the cattleman replied.

"Oh, I have heard of him, yes," Careca said.

"He forced me to sell the cattle to him!" the cattleman revealed.

"How did he do that?" the curandeiro asked.

"Pressure, sir. He used a lot of pressure. He even went to see my bankers," the cattleman said.

"Oh, I see," the curandeiro nodded.

"He knew I had a loan there which I wasn't servicing regularly," the cattleman revealed more.

"Mmmm mm. I see," Careca said.

"I want you to punish him," the client begged.

"And what kind of punishment do you suggest?" Careca asked for clarification.

"You see, I have thought about it. But you tell me if I'm wrong. I brought with me the hairs taken from the different types of cattle that I had. I had zebo, ankole, boran, congoni, *et cetera* all types of cattle!" the client said.

"Ah, I see. But that is a demanding job," the curandeiro hinted.

"No problem," said the cattleman, as he counted another batch of notes and handed them to the curandeiro. "That should do it, my good sir."

"Indeed! Let us see… Wait outside for a while," the curandeiro ordered.

The man went out. It was a warm night. The mosquitoes were buzzing around his ears, forcing him to swat away at them even though he could not see them. Were they guards of the curandeiro?

Inside, Careca fetched a small black earthen pot into which he put a round smooth pearl, a hairy root of a plant, two cowry shells - a bivalve and a tigris, a broken tooth of a warthog, a piece of ivory, a small fibre string and the scary skin of a cobra. He put a little water into the pot and balanced it on the fire. Then he called in the cattleman.

"Where are the hairs?" the curandeiro asked.

They were in a small cloth purse that the man carried in his old Gladstone bag. He opened it.

"Here we are," he said, as he passed the cloth purse to Careca. There were white, spotted, brown, black and striped hairs. The curandeiro put them in the pot and covered it. Then he turned to the cattleman.

"How many years do you want?" he asked him.

"Five years should drive him out of the place," he said.

"You mean three years, don't you?" Careca suggested.

"Yes, three years," the cattleman agreed.

"Then three years it will be," said Careca authoritatively.

Soon the concoction was ready. He took a ladle and stirred it. Then he filtered a little bit into a small cup. He sipped it and blew it out of the mouth in jets, firstly to the north, then to the south, then to the east and, lastly, to the west. He then gave the cup to the cattleman.

"You are not to swallow anything. Just sip and blow it into the fire," the curandeiro instructed.

"Me?" the cattleman asked.

"Yes, you!" Careca hissed.

It was the nastiest concoction he had ever tasted. If the curandeiro had not taken it, the cattleman would have entertained the thought that he wanted to harm him. He blew it into the fire. Tongues of flames sprung and then died as if doused with water.

The curandeiro turned the pot and took out the fibre string. He closed his eyes and started murmuring things in an indecipherable language. Then he tied three knots on the string and passed it to the cattleman.

"You hold the power in your hands. Each year that passes, you should untie one knot. The cows will procreate only after you have untied all the three knots. Not before. That is a lot of power, do not misuse it." The cattleman took the string and put it in a small purse. "But remember, I have to see that string every six months. You may go." The curandeiro rose to bid his guest goodbye.

Two years, hence Mali Mingi appeared at the home of the same curandeiro. He wanted to know what was wrong with his cows and whether anything could be done about it. The man who had brought him to the curandeiro was well-known to Careca. But neither he nor Mali Mingi knew of his involvement in blocking the course of nature as far as Mali Mingi's cattle were concerned.

"You have come too late, Mali Mingi," he said, after examining the events in his special mirror. "You should treat the disease at the beginning, not at the end. I am not saying that you should treat the symptoms instead of the disease. I'm saying that, in this case, the symptoms and the disease are the same. They should have been taken seriously."

"Are you saying then that there is nothing you can do for me?" asked Mali Mingi in desperation.

"No. With regard to the cattle that were bought two years ago, there is nothing I can do. However, with regard to recently acquired cattle, that I can handle."

"Too few! Too few," Mali Mingi murmured.

"Go and think about it. There is no hurry in Africa," the curandeiro advised.

Six months later Mali Mingi abandoned his farm and his ambition of becoming the biggest cattle rancher in the province.

****

By the time Dona Rosa reached home, she had turned over in her mind all the personal experiences she had shared with her friends and relatives regarding curandeiros. Both Araujo and Benito had not arrived yet. Perhaps they had a longer journey. Perhaps Araujo's illness could not allow a faster pace and, hence the delay in getting home. It was just as well. Dona Rosa began to prepare dinner for herself and her sons.

The visit reminded Benito of the two semi-deaf fishermen of Tete. They had once noticed each other across the street and exchanged their kind of greetings.

Toni: Hello! Senhor Pescador. Are you going fishing?

Pescador: No, I am going fishing.

Toni: OK. I thought you were going fishing.

Pescador: No. Today I am going fishing. How about you? Are you going fishing?

Toni: No. Today I am going fishing.

Pescador: All right. I thought you were going fishing. Bye bye!

CHAPTER FOUR

MARIA

If you tell the curandeiro that you do not eat fish, he will tell you that, that is the problem. You should start eating fish, plenty of fish. If you tell him that you love eating fish, he will warn you against eating fish. Don't touch, he will say. When you tell him that your wife and your mother have quarrelled, he will tell you to beware of a simmering mother-in-law-daughter-in-law tug-of-war.

"Don't ever get caught in such a tug-of-war," he will say.

That appeared to be the conclusion of Antonio Phiri, Araujo's curandeiro. Araujo was to steer clear of any such tug-of-war.

"But it's over, is it not? Maria has gone to her people," Araujo said.

"Physically, she has gone," replied Antonio. "But her anger has not. Her spirit of revenge has not gone. And another thing…her mother will want to avenge her daughter. That is what you are up against. That is what we must deal with," the curandeiro said.

"Avenge for what?" Araujo dug for answers.

"When Maria returned to you she knew that she could not conceive anymore. They had told her as much at the hospital and her curandeiro had confirmed that some vital organ of procreation had been damaged. They attributed this to your negligence. Maria was therefore given medicine to ensure that you, too, were disabled and would not be able to make a woman pregnant. That was her mission. When it was accomplished, she went home, pretending to have been abused by your mother." Antonio Phiri paused for this message to sink. Araujo made some uneasy movements of the head but said nothing.

Benito was clearly shocked. Was he hearing right? Maria wanted to castrate Araujo, was that it? She returned to him to make sure that he was crippled? Villain! She was a villain! He railed in his heart.

Antonio Phiri wanted to hear how Araujo was actually feeling. While Araujo explained, the curandeiro was making a mental assessment. Yes, the man had lost substantial weight. Yes, he often contracted itchy skin infections. Yes, he had warts and sores that were not healing properly, not to mention the irritating dry coughs that went on and on.

"I have almost become lethargic," Araujo concluded.

"You are a lucky man, in a way," said Antonio Phiri. "I have just come from Malawi. Some of the ingredients I need are not available here. I had gone to replenish my stock!"

Six different types of herbs were cooked in a small pot to produce syrup, which was put in a coconut cup. Some blood of a cock and a piece of roast 'mpheta[4]' were added and Araujo had to drink the concoction. Two incisions were made, one on the left side of the navel and one on the right side, and a drug was smeared on each of them and the blood let to clot. He was then asked to go out of the hut with his back to the door. Once outside, he was asked to go round the hut and return inside.

"You wanted to know whether Maria would return to you. Well, now you know. She left a good man. She will never find another one. Nor will she have any influence over you, for she has no power at all," the curandeiro said.

The trip around the curandeiro's house was instructive. Araujo saw relics of dead animals: bones, hair, skins, hooves, nails; fetishes and amulets and what may have been a sex totem and other numerous small bundles of dried roots and pieces of wood. There were many pots and gourds and calabashes arranged haphazardly around the eaves of the house.

This was the headquarters of Antonio Phiri, friend or foe, satisfier of determinate necessities, providing a link between the natural and the supernatural, the material and the spiritual and between the visible and the invisible, through a scrupulous adherence to the teachings of his predecessors.

---

[4] Mpheta - siNyanja term for the destructive quelea bird that grain farmers all over fight against all the time, especially the red-billed species.

The power, the will and the spirit of a curandeiro reposed here in this venerable dwelling. Long live Araujo's curandeiro!

****

Maria arrived home a changed woman. Along the way, she had opened all the compartments of her memory and peered into her misty past. Before she met Araujo, she had fallen in love twice and been pregnant twice but, on both occasions, she had discovered the lie and had promptly aborted the pregnancies. She had wanted to keep Araujo's baby. In fact, she needed to keep his baby. She yearned to keep it. She feared to lose it. And she went on to lose it. And now she had lost Araujo as well. That was cruel fate, very cruel.

The worst of it was that she felt that she was losing control. She wanted to think but she couldn't. She wanted to sing but she couldn't. She wanted to play mental games but her mind was blank. Or perhaps not blank. There was this nagging feeling that she would not reach home. There was a gathering cloud of uncertainty, a lingering doubt about her health. But reach home she did, despite being so downhearted.

****

"He is not only brilliant but very cunning, as well," observed Benito on the way home.

"And dead serious," added Araujo.

"Do you really believe he has the power to silence Maria?" Benito asked.

"Have you any doubts?" asked Araujo.

"No, but, but… well, let's wait and see," Benito replied.

"I would like her to see me one day with my wife and children," Araujo said meditatively. "I would like her to know that her devious plans never worked. I would like to see the shame in her eyes."

"She won't dare face you. She might even run off to Maputo, the city of lights," Benito predicted.

"She won't go anywhere," Araujo said matter-of-factly.

That night Araujo had a disturbing dream. He had been drinking with a fellow he had met for the first time that very evening. They were both sozzled but not completely out. Araujo insisted, actually demanded, that his friend should accompany him so that he may show him his house. This is how the conversation went:

"You see here? This is where I turn left to go to my place," Araujo directed.

"OK. I see it," the friend said.

"And here, no, not here, that light you see there, that is the light on my veranda," Araujo said.

"I see that is the veranda," the friend agreed.

"Watch the step! You see these stairs? They are stairs to my house," Araujo continued.

"Is it very far?" his friend asked.

"Not far, it is up. You go up like this, follow me," he directed.

They struggled up the stairs to the second floor and then found their way to the right door.

"You see this? This is the door to my house. Eh, pal. Where are my keys? I have them somewhere, I know, but where?" Araujo wondered.

"What is that you are holding in your other hand?" his friend asked him.

"Eh, pal. Here they are! I open the door to my house, and here we are! Enter, my friend, this is my house. This is the kitchen. I will surprise you, my friend. You see that beautiful sitting room? That is my sitting room," Araujo said.

"Very impressive!" the friend complimented.

"I don't make too much noise about my house, you see. But it is a real house, you agree?" he asked his friend.

"A real house! Yes," his friend agreed.

"Now I surprise you, come this way. You have not seen my wife," Araujo said.

Araujo opens the bedroom door.

"Yes, this is my bedroom. You see that beautiful woman sleeping on the bed? That is my wife."

"I see!" the friend nodded.

"Not everything. You haven't seen everything. You see that man sleeping with her? That is me! Yes, that is yours truly!" Araujo went on and on.

****

"Remember my words? I knew they were not the kind of people to trust with my daughter. They are primitive, mean and foolish. Don't ever think of going back to them!" Maria's mother was beside herself. Her daughter was a victim of a family conspiracy hatched by Dona Rosa and her sons. She had put a wedge between Maria and her sons. There can be no blinking the fact. She had no compunction whatsoever.

"Her sons are moving about blindfolded and they cannot see that she is behind it all. Somebody has to teach her an all-time lesson. Somebody has to enter that home with a shining blade and cut it to size," she announced to a bewildered Maria.

"Don't worry about me, mother," Maria responded. "I do not need Araujo or any other man for that matter."

"Yes, you do. You shouldn't waste your youth and beauty with nincompoops. You need a nice, caring man of means, who will assure comfort in your home," her mother said.

"What I need is a cure against any such cravings," Maria said contemplatively. "I just need to rest."

It had been a long, dreary journey under a blazing, blinding sun. The ride in the only truck that plied the route had been equally uncomfortable, if not downright punishing. But now, as she sat there listening to her mother, Maria was convinced that it would be a long while before she could be persuaded to enter into a relationship. There was something deep inside that said, 'No, Maria, don't try. You have no time for that.'

****

Araujo woke up sweating like a tired dockworker. His coughing had not improved to any measurable degree. If anything, it had remained stable, with the jolt that was this inexplicable sweating. He had not finished the medicine he was given by his curandeiro, but already he was unsure of its efficacy. Might the sweating be the cause of this creeping exhaustion, this fatigue that kept him in bed for so long? Each day that passed brought on its own share of sluggishness. Each night that passed brought on its own share of fatigue. The coughs compounded the problem. The sweating compelled a loss of his composure and a chain reaction ensued, worst of all, chronic diarrhoea set in.

His mother returned to her curandeiro and his brother decided to check with his own man. They hoped that what one concealed, the other might reveal and lead, inevitably, to the truth of the matter, and a permanent solution for Araujo's problem. Neither one nor the other came up with any beneficent relief. Araujo was taken from one curandeiro to another and each made his own concoction that he claimed would cure the patient and kill the disease. Each made an incision, which he claimed would protect him from further harm.

Without a concoction the patient would go away disgusted by the rip-off. Without the incision the patient would conclude that the treatment was merely perfunctory. In either case, the patient would not in future return to such an incompetent curandeiro. No curandeiro worth his salt would like such a reputation to spread. So they made the concoctions as a matter of course, and the incision as a precaution. At the end of six months, Araujo could boast of a large number of tattoos, which refused to heal normally and cut the picture of a battered, unsuccessful, though struggling, and feather-weight boxer.

By now, Linda had become a regular visitor in Dona Rosa's home. Every other Saturday, she would come home and help with one thing or another. She would also help Araujo in whatever manner her help might be needed. Then, with Benito in tow, she would return to school. Of late, Benito could not afford to be away from home because of Araujo's condition. So Benito would escort her up to her house and return to his brother. He had once or twice broached the issue of marriage and she had told him not to put too much pressure on himself at the moment.

"Don't overburden yourself," she had told him. "Attend to your brother's illness first then we will talk. There's all the time in the world."

"You are not a burden to me," he had responded.

"But then I'm not married to you," she had answered him.

"I love you so much, Linda," he said.

"You will love me less when I am married to you," she answered.

"Never! My love will increase tenfold," he insisted.

"There's not an atom of truth in what you say," she argued.

"There's an ocean of truth in everything I say about you, Linda. Believe me!" he pleaded.

There is a rock that forms the northern boundary of the primary school where Linda taught. It is actually a series of rocks arranged by nature so accurately to resemble the shoulder, neck and head of a monumental person, when viewed at a distance. The teachers and pupils of this school had decided to find a way to get to the top of the rock formation. When they found it and improved on it, the rock became a popular retreat for friends and lovers on the weekends. It was named the 'Juju Rock.' That is where Benito and Linda chose to sit and while away lovers' moments of bliss, every now and then.

"Do you think it's nature that did this?" Linda once asked Benito.

"I don't know what I think. Maybe this is the head of Monomotapa. I hear there are many of them scattered around what used to be his kingdom," Benito replied.

"He must have used slaves to do the job. Are you a descendant of Monomotapa, Benito?" she asked him.

"A direct descendant, if you ask me. Look at my cheekbones. Don't they resemble those of the Juju Rock?" he answered.

"No, they resemble those of Shaka the Zulu!" Linda laughed, and then capped his head in her hands and kissed him decidedly.

The Shaka in him began to stir. The fire of want blazed a trail in her breast. The blood rushed to his limits. He looked around. They were alone on the crest of the Juju Rock.

****

Maria refused to tell her story to anyone else. Her mother was enough. She refused to relate the story to her father and turned down the questions from her sisters. Her neighbours and friends started pouring in to greet her and hear the latest. But they walked away disappointed. Weeks turned to months and still no word from her own mouth about the events surrounding her departure from her relatively unknown husband.

Then the speculation began. Friends who visited claimed to have been let in on the secret.

"The man is impotent," a neighbour told his friend.

"Impotent?" doubted the friend. "I thought she was pregnant the other time."

"Ah, you don't know? That pregnancy was not his."

"The man has HIV/AIDS. That's why she left."

"Is she also infected?"

"She says she tested negative but I don't believe her."

"He has another woman from his tribe. She caught them red-handed. She's filing for divorce."

"Poor creature! She loved him so much. She is heartbroken. It will take a miracle to save her. His mother is a monster!"

"You know her mother never approved of the marriage. She went to see a curandeiro. The marriage can't work. Maria doesn't have a curandeiro."

"His mother does not like Maria. She went to a curandeiro and he tied her womb. Maria came home to have the womb untied. She has already identified a curandeiro."

"Will she go back to him?"

"With a mother like that, would you?"

Then there was the feedback which was concocted, distorted, exaggerated, even malicious. Her neighbours became hostile; her friends became suspicious and her reputation became dishonourable. She retreated into a cocoon. She became paranoid. The stigma, the isolation and the rejection had taken their toll on Maria.

"They are killing me out there," she once told her mother. "Why should I talk to them?"

"But you aren't doing yourself any good, my daughter," her mother replied. "Go and face them every now and again. Then they will learn to respect you."

"I don't need their respect. I don't need their friendship. All I want is peace. Let them leave me alone and I will find peace." Maria needed peace, for her mind was not at ease. When she was in hospital the last time, her mother had got her a prescription and she had bought her some tablets and other medicaments. Maria asked her mother to buy her the same medicine for her.

"What is the matter, Maria?" her mother asked.

"I'm feeling the same way I was feeling that time. Please get me the medicine!" Maria almost cried.

"All right, Maria. Can't it wait until tomorrow?" her mother asked.

"No," shouted Maria. "I need the medicine now! Or tell me you can't buy it and I'll find a way," she fumed.

"All right, all right, Maria. I'll go right away. Let me fetch the money. It's very expensive medicine, you know?" her mother replied.

"I don't care about the expense!" Maria snapped.

"I do," her mother said. "I buy the medicine because it is you, and I love you."

Dona Rosinda left for the pharmacy. Maria rose slowly and went to the window opening out to the beautiful view of the Zambezi River and its seasonal island beaches. It was hot in the house but she could almost touch the cool breeze washing over the faces of the bathers at that time of the day. How she wished she could join them as she had done in the past!

'Don't I have the right to enjoy a bath in the Zambezi waters?' she mused. 'They stigmatise, discriminate and even deny it. They were my friends, so many of them that bathed there in the river. When did I become an enemy?'

CHAPTER FIVE

ARAUJO

"I can't say I'm not scared, Mother," Benito told his mother one morning. "I simply cannot look at those sores in the mouth, those moulting nails, the mole hair, that lanky figure and pretend there is a ready answer somewhere in a curandeiro's bag. What should we have done that we haven't done, Mother?"

"We have to think, son. We cannot abandon him," Dona Rosa answered solemnly.

"Maybe we should take him to hospital, you know, combine forces," Benito suggested. "Maybe there's something that hospitals can do that curandeiros can't. I don't know. I'm just thinking loud. Maybe at the hospital they know of a good curandeiro, who can help."

Dona Rosa had been thinking along the same lines, but was not sure whether she would like to relive the experience. When her late husband was discharged from hospital, they had recommended that she should seek help elsewhere.

"Where is elsewhere?" she had asked foolishly, as it turned out to be.

"Where?" asked the nurse. "You don't know where? Where are you from?" Then continued to say, "We had better talk outside."

Outside, he had given her the names of three curandeiros, who had the reputation of solving some seemingly impossible medical conditions.

She remembered Matacanha, the curandeiro who kept her late husband oscillating between life and death for two years.

"Yes, I think it's a good idea," she told Benito. "Let's try."

At the provincial hospital, the doctors carried out a series of tests, which confirmed that Araujo was HIV positive and that the killer disease AIDS was at an advanced stage.

Unfortunately, it was not fashionable at the time to inform the patient or the relatives that their kith and kin were suffering from the Acquired Immune

Deficiency Syndrome. They mentioned a number of possible diseases and wished that the patient had been brought to the hospital earlier.

"We can give you some pain killers but we cannot guarantee that they will suffice," said one of the nurses.

"I would like to see the doctor," insisted Benito.

"All right, come back at 2.30 p.m," the nurse said.

At three o'clock the doctor welcomed Benito into his room.

"Yes, you wanted to speak to me, I understand," said the doctor.

"Yes. I am his brother," Benito said.

"We are not absolutely sure what it is. We would like to observe him for a few days…then we can form an opinion. But, as you have seen, it is quite serious," the doctor explained.

"Is it AIDS?" Benito asked.

"We do not know for sure," the doctor replied.

Benito was not satisfied. He traced the dresser named Nino, and asked to see him.

"Wait for me outside," said the dresser. "Fifteen or so minutes."

Benito was waiting for him under the luxurious tree shade outside the Casualty Ward. They walked together towards the wards and the surgery.

"Have you been here before?" Nino asked Benito.

"Yes, but I did not go beyond the Casualty Ward," Benito answered.

"You have not been to the medical wards, then?" Nino asked.

"That is true," Benito confirmed.

"And the cancer, TB wards?" Nino asked some more.

"I'm telling you the truth. I have not gone beyond the Casualty Ward" Benito said.

"Come," said the nurse, as he led him into the Men's medical ward.

It was a large, dimly-lit gloomy hall, filled mainly with double-decker metal beds. Benito almost stopped, astonished, when he saw the first patient. He could not make out whether it was a young or an old patient. All that he saw was the anguished stare of misery on what must have been a human face some other time long past. He shifted his gaze from one bed to the other, one face of misery to another, one apparition to another. How tenuous life must be! And yet, how brave the miserable must be! For they were not pleading for pity, these faces, no, they were pleading for understanding. Their skeletal bodies were testimony, if any were needed, that life could inhabit even a stone. They had suffered, were suffering and yet enduring, alive, somehow! But how far were they from getting terrified and overwhelmed?

"This is the medical ward," Nino said softly. "Most of the patients come here on referral from the District Hospitals. But there are exceptions."

"They will be cured?" asked Benito. It was more of a statement than a question really. That was his wish, his hope, even if only for his brother.

"Yeah," said the nurse. "They will all go home in due course."

They moved down the aisle to the end of the ward and Nino talked to a colleague. Then they turned and headed for the door. Back outside the ward, Nino turned to Benito.

"You cannot tell the patient that he cannot be cured, my friend," he said thoughtfully. "You have to be more understanding and tactful with sick people."

"Are you talking about my brother?" Benito asked.

"Not necessarily. There are things that we can do here and there are others that are beyond us. We cannot say that we have the final solution," Nino said.

"Who has?" Benito enquired.

"It is difficult to say. We have had cases that our doctors had, between you and me, given up on. But the individuals are still alive. It all depends on your resources," Nino revealed.

"How is that?" asked Benito.

Nino inhaled deeply and then exhaled almost as much. Whatever he had to tell Benito seemed to be the product of deep thought and consideration.

"The hospital is not the ultimate destination, in every case," he said at last. "Tarsicio de Cocheiro was here. You've heard of him? They took him out every night. He is now at home, a healthy man."

"Who took him out?" Benito asked Nino.

"His people did; that is why I asked you where you come from," Nino stated.

"Listen, Nino. You have to help me. I mean tell me, where did they take him? This is my brother, Nino don't forget that. I'll do anything to get him cured. Please," Benito begged.

"What did the doctor tell you?" Nino asked.

"He doesn't know for sure," replied Benito.

"Nobody knows for sure," said Nino. "Everybody has suspicions, but no one is certain. It could be TB or it could be cancer, but nobody knows. Sometimes we think it is HIV/AIDS then three years later, the fellow is seen still moving around. What kind of AIDS is that?"

Benito shrugged his shoulders. He, too, had his doubts.

"If I were you," continued Nino, "I would consult, you know, consult somebody who can deal with these things the traditional way, maybe. I cannot say he will treat him successfully, but we have the case of Tarsicio de Cocheiro." He paused, took out a pen and a pad and wrote down a name. He passed the paper to Benito. "I wish you good luck, my friend."

"Thank you," Benito said with his eyes glued on the piece of paper.

Matacanha was a familiar name…could he be the one he knew?

After passing a commensurate fee to Nino, it was arranged that Araujo would be taken out at night to consult the curandeiro.

Matacanha received them with mixed feelings. He was happy to see Dona Rosa after such a long time. But he would have been happier if it was not her son that was so gravely ill.

"It is a pity that we are meeting again in such inauspicious circumstances," Matacanha responded, unhappily. "But you can rest assured that I will do everything possible to help your son."

"He is your son, Matacanha," Dona Rosa said appealingly.

"Yes, he is. His father was like a brother to me," he said reflectively. "You have to leave him with me until tomorrow lunchtime."

"We didn't want to bother you so much," she said apologetically.

"We've just agreed that he is my son," the curandeiro said firmly.

By the time they went back to Matacanha's home the next day, he had made Araujo regurgitate all previous treatments by curandeiros and hospitals; he had exorcised the demon that was holding him captive and defenceless, and he had prepared a regimen of medication and diet that he was to adopt for the next few months. Araujo was ready to be taken home. He was not to be taken back to hospital. He was sweating, true enough but this was a different kind of sweat. It was like the sweat of a man who had eaten a whole chicken and drank three cups of chicken soup with hot spices!

They had good news for him, too. While Araujo was at the hospital, there was another patient, an unlikely patient, in the same hospital, in the same ward.

They were all in high spirits throughout the journey home. Araujo had got a shot in the arm, as they say. He felt life throbbing in him, urging him on. Benito had one of his doubts about Antonio Phiri's power silenced. Dona Rosa had proof that her curandeira was 'firmly in control.'

"I can't wait to tell you this, my son. Your problems are finished. Maria is dead!" she announced triumphantly.

Apparently, during the time Araujo was at the hospital, Maria had been admitted there suffering from 'malaria,' as word had it. She had been sitting outside with another patient trying to catch a little sunshine when Dona Rosa, Benito and Araujo entered the male ward. She saw them clearly. But even if they had looked in her direction, they would not have recognised her. She was so thin and had a headscarf on. Upon seeing Araujo, Maria almost stood up and shouted. But she had no strength for that. She watched him walk unsteadily, supported by Benito, into the ward. Then she summoned all the strength that she had left and, with the help of her fellow patient, walked back to the ward and sat on the bed, which she shared with another patient. Her weak heart was pounding away as though she had just completed a marathon race.

'If he is here,' she mused, 'then I have no hope.'

On the night that they took Araujo away to see Matacanha, Maria died in her sleep. Dona Rosa and Benito had learnt about it the following morning before returning to Matacanha's home.

"It is not true," Araujo said after a moment's silence. "It is not true," he repeated quietly.

"It is true," Benito said without betraying any emotion.

Araujo looked blankly at both of them. Then, without uttering another word, he rose and went into his house and into bed.

"I know he loved her; but she hated him," Dona Rosa said resignedly. "She wanted to kill him."

* * * * * * * * * *

"Pull yourself together, Mother," Maria's sister was telling her mother. "We don't know for sure whether it was him or not. Furthermore, nobody has seen him there since, unless he also died the same night."

"She said she saw him," her mother countered.

"Yes, but how do we know? She was so tired!"

That was one week after Maria had been buried at the cemetery. Her mother, Dona Rosinda, had sworn to avenge her by organising, through her curandeiro, the death of one of Dona Rosa's sons. She planned to see him the following day.

"I will not rest until I have done it. Maria's blood must be avenged. Her bones will not rest until I have done that," she swore.

"Mother, you mustn't talk like that," the daughter advised.

"If I don't do it, who will? Your father's keeping mute, like she didn't belong to him. Why should I keep quiet?" She was inconsolably depressed. "They will know they have stirred up a hornet's nest!"

The next day, Maria's mother, Dona Rosinda, was at her curandeiro's home. She narrated her story in great detail. At long last, she came to the point.

"That is why I am here. I want them to know that we know what happened," she concluded. "I want them to pay in equal measure."

"I would like a little clarification, Dona. Who do you say killed your daughter? Is it the mother or the sons or all of them combined?" the curandeiro probed.

"Does it matter which of them did it?" she asked.

"Yes. Otherwise I would not have asked," the curandeiro said. "Is the blame on one person or is it to be shared?"

"OK," Dona Rosinda answered. "I am here to find out. But I'm sure they did it."

"Now we are getting close to it. You are here to find out. Otherwise, frankly, I was going to say that you are placing the matter beyond my reach," the curandeiro stated.

"All right, sir. The matter is in your hands," Dona Rosinda said as she fetched a handkerchief, wiped the sweat on her face and folded her hands in below her breasts. 'You can't take away a curandeiro's power,' she thought. 'You don't tell him what to do. You pay him and submit to his power. He tells you what has to be done. He demands of you only total obedience.'

One and a half hours later, Dona Rosinda walked out of her curandeiro's house clutching her handbag rather tightly. The instruments of magical and spiritual power over life were lodged therein.

On the seventh day, she was to await the curandeiro outside her gate at six in the morning. In the meantime, she was to ensure that no stranger entered her compound unaccompanied by her or a trusted member of her family. She was to wear the charm that she was given throughout the period. That was the only link between her and the curandeiro. The contents of one of the small containers were to be poured sparingly and discreetly round the compound within the next two days.

On the appointed date at six in the morning, her curandeiro and an assistant stood at the gate. She invited them in.

"I was not coming to visit you, Dona Rosinda. I have a job to do. Come with us, if you don't mind." He had an impala horn, which he kept close to the ground, as they went round the compound. Then all of a sudden, the curandeiro and the assistant stopped. In front of them were two snakes, one bigger than the other. "We've got them," the curandeiro said, "the two conspirators."

Apparently, the assistant was a snake charmer. He went to work. Within ten minutes, both snakes were in his bag.

"The big one is the mother; the small one the son," the curandeiro explained to Dona Rosinda.

"I want the son," she said. "I want her son, so that she can feel the way I'm feeling. Nothing but the son."

"You have him in that bag, Dona, you have him. And the woman, what shall we do with the woman?" the curandeiro asked.

"I want her to witness. I want her to live the experience!" she replied.

"Very well, so it will be. Set her free, Maenda, will you?" The assistant went to the gate and released the larger snake. It did not look back. It slithered away into the neighbouring shrubs, towards the river.

"Just wait for the news," the curandeiro told Dona Rosinda.

Dona Rosinda opened her bag and paid the balance. The curandeiro and his assistant disappeared as they had come, with the snake in their bag. The waiting game had begun.

Dona Rosa decided to leave Araujo alone for some time. After all, he was now fitter than usual. And his brother, Benito, was keeping him company. She had to worry about other fairly important matters, one of which was to make sure that her grain was sold and converted into liquid cash. The other was to make sure she consulted her curandeiro to seek ways of averting the expected retaliation from Dona Rosinda. She knew Dona Rosinda would not take anything lying down, as the saying goes. She would fight back. Dona Rosa was not to be caught flat-footed. She had been a cautious woman all along. She would not fail now. No, not now. Of all the time, not now!

A few days later, she was at her curandeira. "You appear to have touched a live wire," the curandeira said to her. "But don't worry. We have done it before. We can do it again. All that is needed now is patience."

Protective reinforcements were prepared and cast to the four cardinal points of the compass.

"That will take the wind out of her sails," her curandeira said confidently.

Dona Rosa's waiting game had also begun.

Araujo and Benito were discussing recent events one afternoon at home.

"I wonder how much longer this will go on?" Araujo asked Benito. "Everybody is fighting everybody else."

"Come on, brother," Benito said. "You must put your best foot forward and keep moving."

"But can't you see? This war is sapping vital energy. Look at this house. When do you suppose I will finish the extensions?" Araujo said.

"Don't worry about the house now. Even the space, it is not all being put to use," Benito enlightened.

"OK. So we fight them and they fight us. Who will win in the end?" Araujo asked.

"Look, the real issue is not about winning. It is about losing. We fight because we don't want to lose. The fear of losing fuels the war," Benito responded.

"But, in the long run, don't we all lose?" Araujo persisted.

"Tell me. Who is interested in the long run?" Benito asked.

"Sometimes I wonder," Araujo reflected. "If our fathers had not fought for our independence, would our generation have taken up arms and gone into the forests? I really wonder! And now that the land has been liberated people cannot develop it and build decent houses for fear of bewitchment by envious neighbours and relatives."

"But bewitchment is for real. What do you want them to do? Take all their hard-won savings and throw the money into the drain?" Benito asked.

"I suppose not," Araujo said. "So the fourth millennium will find us still living in hovels!"

"What do you want? What are you looking for?" Benito asked his dear brother.

"I want peace and quiet. I want you and me to live in harmony. I want mother to concentrate on her farming. I want you to marry Linda and bring up a family, without fear of curandeiros and curandeiras," Araujo answered.

"Do you really mean that?" Benito asked.

"Yes, I do. I need a rest. I don't want to join the hate squad!" Araujo reassured his younger brother.

Benito hugged his brother. This was the most satisfying chat they had had as adults. Araujo, though sickly, was a magnanimous individual. Society had its priorities upside down. But who was there to say that he was right?

"Brother, do you feel strong enough to visit my friend?" asked Benito.

"There is no need for that. Look, who's at the gate?" Araujo said.

"Fancy that!" exclaimed Benito as he noticed Linda at the gate. "Hello, Linda, my love! How thoughtful of you to pay us a visit...just as we were thinking of you!"

Linda joined them under the tree shade.

"Araujo, you look so fine," Linda said. "Beni, you must bring him to school one of these fine days. Where's your mother?"

"Busy as usual, fending for her sons!" said Benito.

"It's high time the sons started fending for themselves," replied Linda.

"What have you got in that bag?" asked Araujo.

"Sorry, I almost forgot," she said. "There aren't any pineapples at the market at the moment. I only managed to buy some bananas and oranges. Here!"

"And some tangerines," observed Araujo. "I like tangerines. Thank you very much."

"I'll have a banana," said Benito, "and then I'll tell you something."

"Tell us now. What is it?" Linda wanted to hear right away.

"I've not tasted the banana yet... Yes, it's sweet, very sweet. Now, listen to this... Madalena is preparing chicken on the grill for her boss and her colleague observes:

'You will never perfect that particular dish!'

'Why should I perfect it?' Madalena retorts. 'Don't you know he never leaves anything for us?'"

"I also have one for you," said Linda. "A fellow was once arrested and taken to court for being drunk."

'Who arrested you?' the judge asked.

'Two policemen, your honour.'

'For being drunk?'

'Yes, your honour, both of them.

Contrary to expectation, Araujo's health did not follow the predicted path. One day he would be jolly and confident. The next day he would be moody and nervous. One day he would be cheerful and vibrant. The next day he would be withdrawn and quite under the weather. Occasionally, he was low; on the brink of a breakdown.

One Sunday morning, his mother brought him breakfast, made according to the curandeiro's regimen. She sat a little distance away, peeling some beans. Benito, who had been taking a bath, joined them in a family chat. Eventually, the subject changed to curandeiros.

"Tell me, Mother. In all your dealings with these people, have you ever heard of a curandeiro who blamed any problem on an animal or thing?" Araujo asked.

"Any problem like what?" his mother asked for clarification.

"Like death, disease or accident," Araujo clarified.

"I don't know what you mean," his mother said.

"There must be deaths, which are natural; accidents, which are caused by animals; or diseases, which are caused by germs," Araujo persisted.

"You want to know whether a curandeiro can classify such an occurrence?" his mother asked.

"Yes, precisely," he agreed.

"So what is the question?" his mother asked.

"I want us to stop this war with Maria's family," Araujo said.

"We did not start it. Tell them to stop it. But what is going on? Listen, my son, they are fighting us tooth and nail and claw. If we don't fight back, we are finished. You ought to know that. Look at what they are doing to you! Oh, you think I am the villain, because I fight back? I'm fighting evil. I'm fighting to keep you alive. Don't you want to stay alive? No, my son, I cannot stop it. Let them stop it. Do you know how many curandeiros they have consulted because of you? Tell him, Benito; tell him this is not a joke. You are all that I live for. I can't ever let you go. Over my dead body!" Dona Rosa fumed.

****

By then, it was almost public knowledge that the two families were at war. Both Dona Rosa and Dona Rosinda had seen to that. The only missing tag

69

was an official declaration. The slightest cough in the enemy camp was monitored and relayed to allied forces and vice versa. The relaying mechanism was such that by the time the recipient got the news, a transmutation had occurred. Coughs became cancer and malaria became AIDS, and so on.

When a few weeks later Araujo was bedridden for a week, Dona Rosinda celebrated. A certain tout had told her, that he had died at home. She was so happy that she even boasted to a friend that her curandeiro had arranged the death of a prominent person working with some whites to clear anti-personnel land-mines.

When Dona Rosinda's husband died in a motor accident on the Beira-Chimoio Road, Dona Rosa had her sweet revenge. She was convinced that it was the work of her curandeiro. Araujo did not even want to hear the news. He had lost all interest in the war memos, as he called the gossip.

Dona Rosinda panicked. She had to avenge herself against Dona Rosa at all costs. She changed her curandeiro and consulted an old man reputed to be absolutely lethal, if one paid the right price.

Dona Rosa had also gone for reinforcements.

"Don't break your back over the issue," her curandeiro had told her. "Dona Rosinda knows she is losing the game. She will stop. Our missiles are in place."

"I just wanted to be sure," she had responded.

A few days later, Benito was down with malaria. It was not responding to the usual treatment. Dona Rosa went to the curandeiro. In the meantime, Linda appeared with some tablets she had bought in town. Benito took a course of the tablets and within three days, he was out and about, although he had lost some weight. He did not tell Dona Rosa about the tablets. All the time Benito was sick, Araujo was at his side and had said to him, "I'm not a very happy man, Beni. But I hope you will find real happiness, one day. If not here, perhaps somewhere else."

"Why do you say that?" Benito had asked.

"Because I care," he replied. "Your malaria will go away. My illness is not going away. It is still there. It's like a gathering storm. Clouds come and pass, but there are more clouds where they are coming from."

"But what is it, Araujo? What do you think it is?" Benito asked.

"I don't know. Perhaps you can also tell me. If it was AIDS, would I still be here?" Araujo asked.

"Then you will be here a long time. I can't imagine life without a brother. Tell me, do you still think she loves me in this condition?" Benito asked his brother.

"That woman simply adores you. I don't know what you gave her!" Araujo reassured his younger brother.

"I just gave her all my love." Benito said.

Once again, the school holidays were at hand, and Linda wanted to introduce Benito to her parents. They left on Friday morning and arrived in Tete that evening. They booked a room at Hotel Kassuende, had dinner at Domino and danced at the Desportivo. They got up at ten on Saturday morning and, by noon, they were at her mother's house in the Josina Machel estate. It was a tumultuous welcome they received from her sister, Lilian, and her brother, Miguel. Naturally, her mother was more cautious. She eyed the young man intently and then accepted a peck from him, as if she feared he might bite her.

"So this is Benito," she said as if she had read the name in a postcard. "Welcome. Lunch will be ready in a moment."

It was sumptuous and delicious and Benito loved it. Linda's brother and sister made sure that he ate a lot of food. Rural people were supposed to have a little more room in their stomachs than town people. Benito lived up to expectation, although reluctantly, he did not want to betray himself with overenthusiasm. Deep down he knew that he needed the richer, greasier urban food that was alien in Culamawe.

After lunch, they went to La Bamba with friends of hers. It is there that Benito gave her an engagement ring. They dined at her cousin's and went back to the Desportivo for the midnight dance. Sunday was quieter. Her aunt hosted lunch and the introduction ceremony, and her mother cooked dinner. Her brother and sister insisted on taking them to Pemba - the teenagers' Sunday joint.

On Monday morning, it was all smiles as an exhausted Benito bade them farewell and was on his way back to Culamawe. Actually, they had wanted him to stay a few more days in Tete. He was a jolly and likeable person.

But something told him all was not well at home. He felt uneasy. He told Linda what was on his mind. She understood. She let him go.

His mother spotted him at the gate and almost ran to meet him and hastily said, "You see why I need you here? He is sick again. He is dreaming too much! He can't eat; can't drink. He keeps calling your name," she told him rapidly, as they hurried to Araujo's room.

"I'm here brother," he said holding his hand. "What's the matter? Tell me. How are you feeling?"

"It's the stomach. It's hot, hot like pepper. What should I do?" Araujo asked him.

"Have you eaten anything?" Benito asked.

"I can't. I'll throw up!" Araujo whined.

"Did you take any medicine?" Benito asked another question.

"It's burning my insides. I can't take it!" Araujo complained.

"Mother, do we have any porridge?" Benito asked his mother.

"Yes, the porridge is there. It needs to be warmed," their mother responded.

"OK. Warm it just a little bit and bring it," Benito ordered.

On the advice of Linda, he had bought some painkillers. He wanted to try them but he did not want mother to know. When she was gone and they were alone together, he decided to let Araujo know.

"I've brought some medicine I want you to try. I will put it in the porridge. Please try to eat the porridge. Medicine reacts negatively on an empty stomach. Promise to try," he urged Araujo.

"I'll try," Araujo promised weakly.

CHAPTER SIX

DONA ROSA

The medicine reduced the pain considerably but the vomiting continued. Then the pain recurred with regular frequency. The regimen that the curandeiro had ordered became ineffective and, in fact, counterproductive. As soon as he saw the food, Araujo started to retch. Matacanha had to be brought to Culamawe. But all his efforts were in vain. He promised to come back, but he did not do so. Two other curandeiros came in, including Antonio Phiri, but Araujo's condition only worsened.

By the time he died after a long struggle with the killer disease HIV/AIDS, Araujo was sick and tired of being sick and tired.

Dona Rosa was broken. Benito was heartbroken. The Vanga family was in mourning!

Dona Rosa did not know where to turn. She had tried all the curandeiros within her reach. Yet they had not saved her husband, Eugenio, or her two sons, Gaspar and Araujo. Now there was only Benito. Who would protect him?

She had known where to look for help. She knew the twists and turns of the world of traditional African medicine. She knew many practitioners. She knew the kind of clientele. She knew the system.

But it had failed to protect her beloved ones. The medicine had failed her. The practitioners had failed her. And the system had failed her. There was nobody to trust. There was a vacuum, a chasm, and an abyss. She had led for so long. Now she was ready to be led.

Benito was Dona Rosa's pampered son. He had known no difficulties, no problems and no want. He had a strong mother. She solved problems, she took responsibility and she faced the unknown. She was mother and father to him.

But Araujo's illness had taught him something that perhaps, she wasn't unimpeachable, irreproachable. There was even a suggestion of sinister motives in her actions. He was unsure of himself. How was he to comport with her?

True, they cried together, sorrowed together over the death of Araujo. But his sorrow was not shared with her. It was his own loss of a dear brother, a dear friend, and his closest comrade. He was not mourning Araujo, the son of Dona Rosa. He was mourning a part of himself.

He needed guidance. Linda was away in Tete, and Araujo was gone. Dona Rosa, his mother and erstwhile 'rock of ages' in his eyes, could no longer help him.

He went to his curandeiro and related the whole history of his family, as he knew it. When he was finished, the curandeiro asked him questions, many questions.

He wanted to know how his mother spent her time. He wanted to know if she had a man friend, a companion, a man she confided in. Did she talk a lot about his father? Did she talk about other men? Did she talk about marriage? What was her view of marriage? Did she advise the children about marriage? Who to marry? When to marry and how to keep the wife happy? Did she give presents to Maria before they got married? Had she given any to Linda? What did she want for herself? He wanted to know all these things.

Then abruptly he stopped. He looked at Benito, and then he looked down. He looked at him again and, again, looked down. Then he fixed a stern gaze on Benito. "What I'm about to tell you will not please you, but you did not come here to be pleased. It will not comfort you. It may not satisfy you. But you are a man. You can dodge the truth, but it will catch up with you. You can hide the truth, but only for a while. If truth will make you cry, then tears are better than laughter, in the eyes of those that seek the truth."

He looked at the mirror in front of him. He rotated it and turned it in several angles. He resumed the severe gaze. "Only she can explain where she is leading to, for she alone knows. She knows you will run away with Linda and she will not let that happen. She is the culprit. I cannot say more. My instruments will reveal no more!"

74

Benito wanted to ask something but the curandeiro raised his hand. "Can't you see, you are next?" asked Curano Mbabane.

Whilst still on holiday, Linda decided to consult a doctor to find out why she was experiencing nausea just before meals and also in the mornings. Some tests were made and the next day the doctor told her that she was pregnant. "Do you know who is responsible?" he asked Linda.

"Yes, he's my boyfriend," she replied.

"Is he around?" the doctor asked.

"No. He doesn't live here," she responded.

"When you next come to the clinic, I would like to see him," the doctor instructed.

"Is there a problem?" she asked.

"No. Just routine check," he said.

He made out a prescription and Linda went off to buy the medicine. At the chemists, Linda was shocked to find that the prescribed medicine included tablets she thought were given to people who had tested positive for HIV/AIDS. She couldn't believe that she was one of them. She went back to the hospital.

"It's just a precaution," the doctor told her. "I am still studying the tests and I have not reached any conclusions yet. No need to worry. But take the medicine all the same. And remember to bring your boyfriend next time."

Linda went back to school a confused woman. She was pregnant for sure. She had missed her monthly period. Even her mother had noticed the nausea and told her as much.

What she could not believe was that she was HIV-positive. The doctor did not confirm it, but he did not give her a clean bill of health.

What did that mean for her, for the baby in her womb? How did she get the virus? Was it through Benito, the wonder boy of Culamawe? Was it one of her other friends from Tete?

Linda's mind drifted to her friends, both current and recent past. Ever since she had decided to be serious with Benito, she had kept away from other men. Even the one man, who had been close to her she booted, not by telling him to his face, but by dodging him. During the holidays, she just played hard to get, until the last day when there was no opportunity to go to bed with him. But he had been a good friend despite his excessive drinking habits and his notorious womanising. She had witnessed it herself. One time at a party, he had been caught making love to another girl in the adjacent room to the sitting room. He had excused himself to go to the loo and that was good enough reason for him to slip into the next room with the hostess. The party came to an abrupt end, but not before a nasty exchange of words and blows between him and the aggrieved boyfriend.

He had explained to her that all he had done and intended to do was to say goodbye to that girl. She had been his friend and now that she was going to get married and be out of reach, for all time. He had only kissed her, he had explained. Was that so grave a sin that he could not be forgiven?

Linda had forgiven him and gone to bed with him. Did they use any protection, any condom that night? The answer was a clear one: they did not use any protective device.

Where was that friend of hers? Where was Chico? Where?

He had died from malaria that is what people said. But what was the truth? Nobody seemed to die of AIDS! It was always from flu, malaria, cancer or tuberculosis. Why not call it by its real name, HIV/AIDS?

And what is this AIDS anyway? Is it something you catch, just like that, without feeling anything?

While Linda had been waiting to see the doctor, she had seen some magazines and pamphlets about HIV/AIDS. 'Those living with HIV/AIDS are people. They give a face and a voice to this pandemic, making it real for those who have lingering doubt.'

She had wanted to read more but her turn to see the doctor came before she could go far. When she came out of the doctor's consulting room, she was too confused to remember to take a copy. Now she wished she had more information about the disease.

She found a message saying that Benito wanted to see her urgently. He would return that evening. Did she know anything about Benito's brother? No? He passed away. Her informer did not have any details.

She did not have long to wait. Benito was there by five-thirty in the evening. He was crestfallen, forlorn, almost frightened. "He left us, Linda. He left me," he said as he hugged her. "Now I have only you, Linda. You are my only friend, Linda. Araujo is gone forever."

"I'm sorry, Beni. I'm truly sorry. Tell me what happened. Let's go inside," she consoled him.

They went into the house and sat on her bed. He recounted the story tearfully. She listened and sobbed, holding him tightly. When he finished the story, she took out a handkerchief and wiped his sweating, tearful face.

"Beni, there is something I want to tell you." She took his right hand and placed it on her belly. She pressed the area where she supposed the womb should be. "Can you feel anything? I'm pregnant."

"Oh, Linda, that is great! I was wondering when that would happen. Oh, Linda, you turn my sadness into happiness! But how did you know, Linda? How old is he?"

Like most men, Benito expected his first child to be a boy. He felt so proud of his achievement. At the same time, the pregnancy reminded him of Maria. Had she not been equally happy and confident when she discovered that she was pregnant? How life can be misleading! How death can disfigure a mother's expectations, a father's pride.

Linda wanted to tell him about the visit to the doctor's, but she checked herself. That had better wait for another day. She told him about her missed monthly periods and the little swelling in her womb. "We'll have to go to the doctor next month," she told him.

"Certainly. We can go earlier if you want," he replied enthusiastically.

"We shall go next month," she said firmly.

"As you wish, my queen. In fact, I have an important journey to make in the next few days. When I come back we shall get married. I shall arrange everything when I come back. I love you Linda and I love the little fellow in there," he said while feeling her tummy again.

"Where are you going to?" she asked.

"Not out of the country, honey," he replied. "I will tell you everything. Just let me make that trip."

OK. But don't get lost, sweetheart. Don't leave us alone!" she said.

When he got back home Dona Rosa was waiting. "I thought you had decided to leave the old lady alone. Is Linda back from the city? How is she? Did you tell her about your brother?" Dona Rosa asked.

"She is fine. She sends her condolences. She did not know," he replied.

"Your food is on the table. I hope it isn't cold," his mother said.

"Thank you." He went inside and ate his food in silence. "I'm feeling rather tired," he said after he had finished. "I'm going to bed right away," he excused himself.

He had made up his mind. That journey had to be undertaken. It was crucial. It was a matter of life and death. His mother was to accompany him, otherwise the journey would be futile. She was not to know the place until the last possible moment. That would be a fitting surprise for her. Surprise! Yes, the element of surprise was very important for her and perhaps, for him. Even when hunters went into the bush, they hoped to surprise the hunted. That gave them satisfaction. In his case, surprise was good for all those concerned with the issue.

"It is very important for us," he told his mother the following morning. "We have lost three of our beloved in quick succession. It is our duty to find out the problem and to eliminate it once and for all. My informer is very categorical about what should be done. That is why this trip is so necessary. I cannot rest until I accomplish it."

"Is it very far from here? How many days do we need?" she asked.

"Taking the route into account and the fact that we do not know what to expect on the other side, I should say three to four days. One day to travel, one or two days there and one day return journey."

"What do we need to carry?" she asked.

"Nothing," he answered. "Except for clothes and money, we need not carry anything, just clothes and food for a day."

"How are we going, by bus or on foot?" Dona Rosa asked.

"We cannot risk being seen in public. There is too much gossiping going on. We leave by night and return by night. That's my view," Benito informed her.

"Yes, there are too many eyes, groping for scandal. We have to be discreet," Dona Rosa agreed. "When do we leave?"

"Tonight," he replied.

"I'm glad you understand that these matters have to be dealt with urgently. The people at the coast say, 'time and tide wait for no man,'" she said.

"Trust them to know. All those shipwrecks made them learn something," he said coldly.

"You know, son, like me you are very practical. I don't shirk responsibility. If a job has to be done, it has to be done. The earlier the better," Dona Rosa observed pensively. "I will tidy up my things and prepare food for the journey."

Dona Rosa's mind was still preoccupied. There was something intriguing about this visit. Had Benito been planning it for some time? How long? Who had advised him about this trip? Who was to be seen? A famous curandeiro or just one of those friends had mentioned in passing? Could it be a hoax? Could it be a plan to rob them of their money? Or what kind of game is in the making? How many curandeiros did he know? How many had he consulted? Is Linda behind this trip? Is she aware of it? Or is it her curandeiro they are supposed to see? Is she not from Tete, where they claim to know everything about everything and everybody? Is that where they are going? Why the circumspection? Who knows them? Who really cares?

She had all these questions and more, but very few answers, incomplete answers, incongruent answers. Perhaps indifference was the best answer. She became indifferent. Whether the trip was beneficial or not was not important. What did it matter that a trip was not beneficial? A trip is a trip, the benefits notwithstanding.

The important thing - the really important thing - about the trip was that she was not going it alone. She was with her son; a strong, handsome young man. He would be her protector on this trip. Had she not been his guardian since his father died? He is to be guardian for just one trip. That cannot be too much for Benito, she thought.

He was taking up responsibility. He had to do it. Who else was there to do it for him? He had to be his own man. He had to grow up. While Araujo was alive he could not claim to be boss. Now he was the boss. Mother had to listen to him. She had to take his word seriously. She had to accept his advice. She had to walk under his shadow. She was no longer his guardian. She was his charge.

All that Benito needed to carry were a shirt and a pair of trousers. He put them in a small plastic paper bag and Dona Rosa offered to put it in her larger bag. They were to leave at around nine that night. Most people would be asleep by then. Dona Rosa decided to take a longer nap in the afternoon, to avoid feeling sleepy during the journey.

Benito excused himself, saying he wanted to see Linda. Dona Rosa suspected that the trip would either include Linda or at least have something to do with her curandeiro. Instead of going to see her, Benito went to the local canteen and spent the afternoon drinking. He needed to keep his mind focused. One does not go on such trips without strong fortification, he reasoned, especially when the trip is at night and involves one's mother. One has to eliminate all fear and stay focused.

Was the route dangerous? Yes, of course. The African bush is always teeming with danger. From elephant to lion to leopard to snakes to scorpions to mosquitoes, to poachers to robbers to killers! That's the African jungle. That's the route they had to take. That's the risk they had to run.

In the evening, Dona Rosa tried to think aloud. Benito was pretending not to be attentive. She said, "My son, I have been thinking a great deal lately. I cannot say I can be happy here any longer. I do not know whether you can. But I doubt it. That bothers me. The loss of your father and your two brothers, has robbed me of vital energy. I miss them too much. You are my only son and relative left. I cannot afford to lose you."

"But I'm here. You have not lost me," Benito replied.

"I know. Yet I fear that this is not the place to rely on to keep a beloved one safe and sound. It is a rotten place. One cannot move an inch without looking over one's shoulder. It is either a Maria or a Maria's mother or an uncle or some other crank trying to rock your boat," Dona Rosa explained.

"And vice versa," observed Benito.

"I've even thought of selling this place at a throwaway price and setting up a kiosk in town, in another part of the country. There we may be able to live happily if not comfortably. Many people are doing it. They sell potatoes, tomatoes, onions, bananas and other groceries and survive that way," she revealed.

"That's a brilliant idea. We should discuss it when we come back," Benito responded.

At about nine, they locked the doors and the gate and left. Dona Rosa had her bag on her back and a walking stick. Benito had insisted on being armed with an axe and a machete. He had a torch loaded with new batteries. They headed east. The normal routes in the area headed north or west. The mere choice of this direction meant that it was a special trip. Dona Rosa tried to think of an important curandeiro who lived many kilometres away in that direction. Could that be their destination?

Benito led most of the way. He had to use the torch to light up the path. But after about one hour's walking, the moon began to rise and soon produced some extra illumination. It had been pitch-dark, but now it was hazy. The path wound down to and across the streams, then up the slope and across what appeared to be flat brush land. The two travellers were mainly silent, talking only when it was absolutely necessary. Then they came to a place where two paths crossed one another. Benito stopped. "Wait here a minute," he told Dona Rosa. He turned left and moved about twenty paces. "Come this way."

She followed. They walked in that direction for a kilometre or so. When they reached what looked like a forest extending down to a tributary of the great Zambezi River, Benito again stopped. "Wait here," he said again, and followed a narrow path towards the thick forest. Then he came back. "It's not that one. Let's go."

She followed him further down the path leading through the forest. Then abruptly he stopped.

"Are you all right?" he asked her.

"Yes," she lied. She was frightened. This was far too far from home and far too far into the bush, into the forest.

"No need to worry. We are almost there. I just need to identify the tree," he said. Then sensing that the message was not clear, he added quickly. "The tree marks the entrance to our destination."

A few metres from there he again stopped. "Here we are. Follow me." It was another even narrower path leading to the right.

"Is the bag troubling you? Let me help you with it," he said. This was a dangerous place. She would not allow him to be burdened with her bag. Supposing a lion attacked from ... "No, I'll manage. Somebody lives in this forest?" she asked to drive away her own fear.

"People live everywhere! Excuse me. Take the torch. Move ahead. Let me help myself."

They say when a man is afraid the bladder is the first to suffer. He relieved himself. Nothing strange there. This was the third time he was doing it since the journey began. The pattern was exactly the same as the previous two.

"We just go straight on," he said as he resumed walking behind her. "There are no other turns."

The shadows created by moonlight were turning the forest into a live stage. Was that the shadow of an animal or a person? Was it a tree or something else? It was now becoming eerie. She wanted to tell Benito to take the lead when it happened...the axe split her head in two. She did not even cry out!

CHAPTER SEVEN

BENITO'S TRIAL

The deed was, indeed, quickly done. He dragged the body deep into the forest, away from the vanishing path and left it there- left, that is, his mother's body in the eerie forest for carnivores and worms to devour. Two guinea fowls, disturbed by the unexpected nocturnal interruption, cackled angrily as they shifted their lair. A lone firefly weakly lit the unhappy path just as the clouds paled the moon and erased the smattering of fading stars. The owl watched, dismayed, unable to comprehend.

Benito rushed back to the 'spot' and wiped the axe clean with her 'kanga' cloth. He threw it into the bush. Then he took her bag, his machete and the axe and left - his brain benumbed, his heart pounding, his soul cleansed.

Only when he was a kilometre or so away from his house did Benito consciously wonder what he was going to do, where he was going to hide, if at all he was going to hide.

He chose the turn that led him back home. There he opened his mother's hut. He washed the axe and put it at its usual place. Then he took the clothes out of the bag and put them on the bed. He rummaged through them, looking for money, but there was nothing. She must have carried the money on her person. He took her identity card and burnt it.

He went to his hut and changed clothes. He soaked the ones he had worn for the fateful journey in a basin inside his hut and left, taking only a few items of clothing.

The moon was rapidly descending to the west, as if afraid of the first faint plumes of light on the eastern horizon. Benito, who had so far steeled himself against creeping exhaustion, began to feel the weight of the dreadful events of a sleepless night. Doubt settled in his head, fear in his chest and fatigue in his feet. He shook his head, coughed to clear his chest and doubled his pace, a signal to his aching feet that rest was not a viable option. It was a new rhythm that Benito had subconsciously adopted and his body had to attune itself to it. He was now his own boss, his own protector and his own pacemaker. The only person who could have challenged that assertion had become a part of the decaying African jungle that very night.

He turned to the path that led direct to his only hope. The east had cleared and was preparing to receive the sun, but Culamawe still slept, all except, perhaps, Benito and the versatile curandeiros returning from their shrines and other weird errands.

He walked determinedly, like a man with a mission - a mission whose deadline was fast approaching and whose breach could make him shorter by a head!

He dare not look back, for the spirits of the recently departed were afoot, hoping to snare the unwary, for company, perhaps, to the hereafter. He could almost hear their heavy breathing behind him.

'Whatever the pressure, Benito, do not turn your head, or else you will join them,' a shrill voice in his head said. He had to reach the only man, who could understand, who would understand his predicament- his total solution, after a fashion.

The sun, unbidden, rose, driven by unseen forces or, perhaps, lifted gently by hands we dare not see, like hot coal shedding its orange flames to embrace its dazzling daylight plumes. Then Culamawe also rose, yawned, stretched and tarried with little, but important, morning chores.

As Benito entered the cluster of huts that formed the 'aldeia[5]' where his curandeiro lived, women were already sweeping the compound and lighting the morning fires. Children were struggling to forget their scary unfinished dreams, whilst wiping the stains in their drowsy eyes. Those that had to go for morning classes were frantically pacing about conjuring their best appearance for their critical headmaster.

---

[5] Aldeia - a Portuguese term for village.

"You can't go to school like that," a young woman was telling her daughter. "Look at your hair. Come here, Mani."

"What is that you are wearing?" said another woman. "Can't you see it is torn? Fetch the other one."

"But it's dirty, Mother," the daughter responded.

"Better dirty than torn. Why didn't you wash it yesterday? You have to wash it now," the mother said.

"There is no soap," the daughter protested.

"Yes, there is. Ask your sister," the mother insisted.

"She is asleep," the child said.

"Wake her up. Nisha! Nisha! Wake up!" the mother shouted.

"My class begins at ten o'clock!" Nisha complained.

"So you want to lie in bed until half-past nine? Ridiculous! Wake up!" the mother said.

Benito had stopped. He did not know for how long, but it must have been noticeably long, for the woman turned to him and said, "Good morning! Can I help you?"

"Oh, it's alright. Thank you," he said.

"I don't seem to know you. Are you from here?" the woman asked.

"Oh, yes, the other village. Thank you," Benito said as he hurried away towards his curandeiro's hut.

"I was not expecting you so soon," said his curandeiro, as he greeted Benito. "Sit down."

"I had not planned it either," replied Benito.

"It must be urgent then," concluded his curandeiro. "A stopover, perhaps," he added, eyeing the young man's travelling bag.

"It depends," Benito replied.

"Depends? On what?" the curandeiro asked curiously.

Benito sighed. What did his movements depend on? Had he not been free to move, as he liked? Why did it now have to depend on... on somebody else? The alarm in his heart rose again. But who could answer it?

"It depends on you," he said, with a stutter in his voice.

"Well, then, wait for me. Susanna! Susanna!" the curandeiro called out to his wife.

Susanna appeared at the door. She was a well-built, motherly woman, his wife.

"Include my visitor for breakfast, will you?" the curandeiro asked her.

"Oh, yes, certainly!" she responded.

"Give me a few minutes, son of Vanga, and I'll be with you," the medicine man said to Benito.

Benito said nothing. He merely nodded, barely so, as his host went out. His mind was elsewhere, far away although his body was there, in his curandeiro's hut. His eyes were focused on the wall opposite, maybe farther, for his gaze appeared to x-ray the wall and to follow an invisible path to that 'spot', that spot… He shook his head, closed his eyes and wiped something he knew was not there. He resumed his gaze, seeing nothing.

By the time the curandeiro came back, Benito was fast asleep, on his seat. He went out again.

'Let the man sleep, he must have a reason for it!' he mused.

Benito woke up to find matapa[6], boiled arrowroots, cassava and eggs on the small table in the middle of the room. He must have slept for an hour, he reckoned, for it could not have taken a shorter period to prepare all that food. He knew from experience, his mother was an expert… His mother!

His appetite gave way to nausea, the rumble in his stomach turned into a severe knot that cried out to be untied. His curandeiro found him holding his stomach, his face contorted like he had just eaten a raw scorpion!

"Son of Vanga, what's the matter? Oh, what a mess you are in! Come on, let me… let me…" he said, as he turned Benito's head to take a closer look. "Have you eaten something? Did you swallow something?"

"No," said Benito. "I'm okay. It's just that…" He retched … and retched, till he retched bile. Benito's curandeiro thought it was malaria, and was about

---

[6] Matapa - a Portuguese term for vegetables.

to fetch some ingredients for a medication, but Benito shook his head. It was nothing he said, nothing like malaria.

"So, what is it?" asked the curandeiro. "Let me hear the story… but first let us clear this. Susanna!" His wife came and cleared the mess.

"He has not touched the food?" asked Susanna.

"Leave it there," replied the curandeiro. "He will eat in due course."

She had seen many of his patients in various degrees of discomfort. She had attended to them as a nurse would. In a way, she was the unofficial village nurse. She left the untouched food there on the table.

Benito was slowly regaining his composure and his presence of mind.

"An empty stomach is the enemy of the weak," the curandeiro said. "You had better eat; take your time but eat. I, too, had not eaten. I found you sleeping and I decided to let you rest. Susanna!"

They ate while the curandeiro talked about general matters: his involvement with development, the scaling down of donor-funded projects and the coming Independence Day celebrations.

"You know, son of Vanga… our people have to wake up," he said. "They are sleeping too much, celebrating too much and working too little. Yesterday, we had this meeting to review the goat project. You see, initially, they were given two goats and some chickens. Some of those beneficiaries are complaining that they have not received any money to buy veterinary supplies for the goats."

"Why can't they sell the chickens to buy the medicine for the goats?" Benito asked.

"Precisely! That is what the donor chief said. Otherwise, she said, forget the goats and rear the chickens! And you know what? The people grumbled. Can you believe it? They even asked me to appeal to the spirits for help!" the curandeiro said.

"What did you say?" Benito asked the medicine man.

"Only appeal to the spirits for help after having used all your strength," the medicine man responded. He rummaged through his pockets and took out a letter. He had been invited to a meeting with another donor that was distributing condoms and conducting awareness campaigns for 'this disease.' "Do you think I should attend?" he asked Benito.

"You are the invitee," Benito said.

"That is clear, isn't it?" the curandeiro commented.

"Yes, I mean, what's your stand?" Benito tried to clarify.

"You know my stand as far as condoms are concerned. On the other hand, they are also giving participating curandeiros free razor blades for making our incisions. That is the positive side. They want us to use one razor blade per patient. You see, they say that 'this disease' can also be spread through the use of the same blade."

"Incredible!" Benito said.

"That is why I want to attend. I have to know what they are telling our people and get my share of the blades. In any case, we have been fighting for recognition for so long and the officials have been behaving as if we did not exist. Now, they need us! If I do not attend the meeting, it will still go on. It would give our enemies reason to downplay our role."

"Maybe it is good for publicity," suggested Benito.

"It is crucial; it's a major blow to the doubting Thomases," the curandeiro reflected.

"Will you disclose to them how you treat people?" Benito enquired.

"That is another matter," he said. "What you expect to drop, you hold in your hands. What you hold in your heart, you don't drop. You die with it. Anyway, I guess you are feeling better now. Can we begin?"

Benito looked down. He had been comfortable discussing general matters. Now he had to bare his heavy heart, and that weighed even heavier with him. Where was he to begin? And where was he to end? A sombre cloud of emotion swept over him...through him, as he ran over the events of the previous week.

"I did it," he said finally, "as you advised me."

"You did what?" the curandeiro asked.

"I... I sent her ...home...to her people," he said hesitantly.

"Sent who to her people?" the medicine man asked.

"The enemy," Benito said cryptically.

"The enemy?" the curandeiro asked utterly confused.

"Yes," he said.

"To her people?" he asked seeming to understand now what his client was talking about.

"Yes," Benito said.

"Living or dead?" the curandeiro asked, needing to know the specific details.

"Her...her ancestors," Benito said.

"Your ancestors?" the curandeiro asked.

"Yes," he said.

"You sent her, or you had her sent?" the curandeiro kept probing.

"It's all the same," Benito said weakly.

"Is it?" his curandeiro asked.

"I...I sent her. Alone I did it," he revealed.

"When?" was the next question thrown at him.

"Last night...I have not slept a wink," he confessed.

"And you say I advised you to do it?" the curandeiro asked.

"Effectively... that is what I understood," Benito said.

"That is what you understood!" the curandeiro said, almost snappily.

"Yes," Benito said.

"You did not think about it?" the curandeiro asked.

"I did. It was the right thing to do," he responded.

"You decided it was the right thing to do?" the medicine man asked.

"Yes," he said.

"It was your decision, then, wasn't it?" he stated, trying to distance himself from the view that it was he who had planted this seed in Benito`s head.

"Yes," Benito said.

"A legacy of honesty is best of all, son of Vanga. Do not shift the blame, if blame it is. But, courage! If she is with her ancestors, she is safe and in good company. What better company could one wish than to be in their midst? I speak of those whose time has come; but we are not concerned with that now, are we? Awake, son of Vanga, awake! You must bear the burden and bear it well; for you were but a messenger for one whose time had come! And once the time has come, there are no obstacles. The way of our ancestors is always clear," the curandeiro said.

"I understand," said Benito. "But what shall I do now?"

"You must live, son of Vanga, you must live. Where is your woman?" he asked Benito.

"Where she should be - at school," Benito said.

"Does she know?" the curandeiro asked.

Benito shook his head.

"Good. Silence of a kind does the trick," the curandeiro enlightened.

"I do not understand," Benito expressed his ignorance.

"You will, son of Vanga. Women are by nature fickle and irresolute. They think with their tongues," the curandeiro said.

"I should not tell her, then?" Benito asked.

"Not even if she says she loves you to death," the curandeiro advised.

"I love her so much," Benito said.

"That is only 'so much', no more. Let her stand less between you and the sun. You need a clear view of your destiny, all the time," the curandeiro said.

"I cannot go to her yet," said Benito. "I'm not sure I could withhold…"

"There's no hurry. We'll talk some more," the curandeiro said to him.

They talked a great deal more for Benito was a hungry man - hungry that is, for knowledge. His curandeiro was an untapped fund of knowledge. Benito coaxed him into unveiling his great mind and reservoir of knowledge of traditional medicine.

"For years they ignored us, vilified us and even banned our activities," said the curandeiro. "They were busy embracing so-called Western medicine. Now, they want to know what we know, but are not willing to pay for instruction. They are poachers!"

One thing that bothered Benito was the curandeiro's standard incision. His late brother, Araujo, had so many of them made by various curandeiros he consulted. Many of those refused to heal properly. He, Benito, himself, had a few. What was the reason behind making the incisions?

"The only incision I can think of," said Benito, "short of a surgical one to remove a foreign body, is circumcision."

"You want to become a curandeiro?" the curandeiro asked.

"No; but I want to know," Benito said.

"Circumcision is not only a rite of passage and/or religious observance for many communities. It is also a precaution against venereal diseases. It is important for a man to experience pain at an early age, just like a woman experiences pain at childbirth. Both teach a lesson: there is a limit to the amount of pain one can inflict on others. Other incisions have their justifications. It is a long story," the curandeiro explained.

"Can all of them be justified?" Benito asked.

"If you cannot justify the making of an incision, don't make it! That is my principle," The curandeiro responded.

"How does one know whether the medicine smeared onto an incision is wholesome?" Benito kept searching.

"The same way one determines that the oral medicine is wholesome," the curandeiro said. "Is she teaching you the white man's medicine?"

"It is no longer the white man's medicine. They are calling it conventional medicine. But no, she doesn't teach me any medicine," Benito said.

"Does it include Chinese medicine, this conventional medicine?" the medicine man asked.

"I doubt it," Benito said.

"What do you do when she is not teaching you to lie?" the curandeiro asked.

For the first time since the death of his brother, Benito laughed. "I'm not telling you any lies, when I say she does not teach me to lie. But, yes, we spend time arguing and joking."

As a matter of fact, Benito had a joke for his curandeiro. A rich landlord had decided to spend two weeks up-country with his wife. While there, she fell seriously ill and rather than return to the city, a doctor had been summoned urgently. The doctor prescribed a drug, which was in powder form.

'Do you have a pair of scales with you?' the doctor asked.

'What for?'

'It is most important that the dose should neither be too strong nor too weak,' replied the doctor.

'Oh, yes! I have a scale that I use to measure pieces of gold and bars of precious metals.'

'Excellent! Just to make sure there is no mistake, mix in a bottle of water a quantity of the powder equal to a ducat of gold and give her to drink.'

Two days later, the doctor returned to the landlord's country home only to find that the patient had died.

'This is utterly unbelievable,' he said, 'because my cure is totally infallible. Unless, of course, you did not follow my instructions.'

'The proof is the empty box,' said the landlord.

'How is that? You gave her the entire lot?'

'Yes, in two bottlefuls.'

'You made a grievous mistake!' said the doctor.

'Didn't you tell me that I should give her the weight of a ducat? Since I had no ducat of gold, I put on the scale three crowns, which make up one ducat.'

The curandeiro was very impressed. He had one for his patient. A man from Mutarara was fishing along River Zambezi, but had as yet caught nothing.

'How the devil do you expect the fish to bite, if you don't have a bait on the hook?' asked a colleague.

'Look, you mind your own business. If the fish want to bite, let them bite. If they don't want, it's their problem. I'm not here to trick anyone!'

"May I tell you one more?" asked Benito.

"Oh, yes, go ahead," the curandeiro said.

A pastor had asked a parishioner why he drank so much every day.

'It is to drown my sorrows,' replied the parishioner.

'And have you succeeded?'

'No, I have not.'

'Why not?'

'Because my troubles know how to swim!'

"Talking of troubles," said the curandeiro, "have you considered...?"

They discussed in detail the problem that Dona Rosa's death presented and how Benito was to handle the potentially volatile situation.

Two days later, Benito left before dawn, that is, after parting with a handsome sum for his curandeiro.

He took a route that eventually joined the rugged pot-holed Tete-Culamawe dirt road, several kilometres away from home. He then hailed a pick-up that was going to Culamawe. At seven o'clock in the evening, he was standing outside her door.

Linda took him in sweetly as always, but there was something missing. His usual charm and spark was gone. She thought she knew why and so she accepted his new demeanour without question. He had lost a dear brother, his only brother and that was something that smote him deeply. She had to understand and console him, while gently pressing the point that the dead must give way to the living. "How was the journey, honey?" she asked.

"Ok, it was alright, but tiring," Benito said.

"I can see that," she said. "You need a rest, at least two days."

"I feel like I need a week," he said.

"Then take a week," she said. "That would be okay with me. How about the old lady?"

"She will be alright," he said.

"You sure?" she asked.

"She went to Inhambane to inform her relatives what happened. She had to go; otherwise she would have broken down completely," he told her.

"Poor woman, she needed someone to really comfort her; someone who would understand her grief. I guess it's different, the grief of a mother. Poor Benito, you must feel terribly lonely. Why didn't you go with her?" she asked.

"I've never learnt to like them," he said. "They shunned us when Dad died and when Gaspar died, they did not even send a word of condolence. If they had showed any concern then, I might have learnt to like them. Now, I can't tolerate them; I can't, I just can't!"

"Ok, Benito. Don't get upset. Stay here with me. I love you Benito, truly I do," she said, trying to calm him down.

"They poisoned my mind, Linda, they did. They said my mother was a witch. I didn't believe them, but I became guarded about my mother. I obeyed her. I respected her, but I never loved her. I couldn't," Benito ranted.

Linda was getting alarmed. Why was he speaking of her as if she no longer existed? Was he getting confused, or had something grave occurred? She looked at his face, at his eyes, looking for a clue. He looked pained, agitated, afraid and almost nervous. Surely, this must be a new crisis that he is going through! "What happened?" she asked, horrified.

Benito grabbed her, unusually roughly and kissed her passionately as he drew her closer to him. "I love you, Linda," he said, in a shouted whisper. "I have done it for you."

"Done what?" she asked him.

"We are free to marry now. I can marry you anytime now! Oh, Linda, I love you. How is the little one?" He went on and on. Linda pushed him away gently. He was so excited. She had never seen him in this kind of crazy mood.

"What have you done?" she asked fearfully.

"I did what I had to do. There was no other way. It had to be done," he went on.

"What had to be done? I just don't understand you! What are you talking about?" Linda was clearly confused.

"Sit down, Let me explain. You see…"

"I don't believe it!" shouted Linda when he told her that he had killed his mother.

"Listen, Linda. You have to listen to me. She was your enemy. She wanted to kill you. She wanted to consult curandeiros. She killed Araujo; she killed Maria; she killed…"

"Stop it! Stop it, Benito. Araujo died from AIDS and you know it. And let me tell you. It is quite possible that you have it and your baby here has it. I went to the doctor and he said I should take you along next month, so that he can do some tests on you. And now you are telling me that you have murdered your own mother? I don't believe it, Beni! Where is she? Where is her body? That woman loved me!"

"She is dead. Listen, all this talk about AIDS is nonsense. It is a creation of the white man's mind. I have listened carefully to people who know. It is total bewitchment. You get bewitched and you blame it on AIDS. I tell you

Araujo himself told me what was killing him. He blamed her. He blamed her for killing my other brother, Gaspar. She spent a lot of money on curandeiros. What made me do it is that she told me that I couldn't marry you. She was planning to sell the farm and take me with her to another part of the country. She said that you were rotten. Everything is rotten. I couldn't stand it, Linda. I had to act. I had to free myself to be with you always," he said.

"No, Benito, you killed your mother. I don't want anything to do with you. I don't want..." she said, sobbing.

"Can't you see? I love you, Linda. Don't you love me? You don't love me? Is that what you are saying?" he was getting desperate.

"If you have killed your mother, then I don't want to have anything with you!" Linda had heard enough.

"But I did it for you! Come on Linda, don't be unreasonable. I did it for you. I love you. What do you say to that? That you now don't love me?" he asked.

"No, I don't!" she said curtly.

"Yes, you do. You love me, you bitch. You love me. You loved me from the very first day. Say you love me... or else... Say it!" he said this as he was growing visibly angry.

Linda tried to shout for help but he put his hand over her mouth and thwarted her effort. A struggle ensued but he soon overpowered her.

"Say it, now! Say you love me! How come I love you and you don't love me? Tell me, Linda!" he was shouting.

Linda struggled to the end. Then she ran out of breath and stopped struggling and lay limp on the bed. Benito still would not take his handkerchief off her mouth for fear she might shout.

"Tell me, Linda! I want to hear from you. Tell me you love me! For I love you too much, Linda. Tell me!" he continued.

There was a knock at the door. The row had reached the ears of one of her neighbouring colleagues. Benito removed his handkerchief from her mouth. He had nearly killed her in his quest to be accepted.

"Linda, are you okay?" shouted the teacher. "Benito, what is happening? Who is killing who?"

"It's all right," Benito answered, in a trembling voice.

"It's not all right shouting and fighting in the middle of the night. What is the problem? Want to kill each other?" the teacher asked, clearly concerned.

"We are not doing anything of the sort. We are just arguing," said Benito.

"Then, don't you argue at the top of your voices. Argue like grown-ups!" the teacher said.

"It's all right, Estevão," Linda managed to say weakly.

"Ok but keep it down. If there's a problem, let me know. Benito, this is a school. We can't allow strangers to intimidate teachers. You hear?" the teacher threatened.

"I'm sorry, man; it's fine," Benito said.

Estevão went back to his house. The nature of bad news infects the bearer. Benito was a man, a man who cried when overcome by emotion. He had killed, nay, murdered his mother. He had come close to killing his girlfriend and their unborn baby. Their lives he now owed to Estevão. Had he not knocked at the door in the nick of time…

He sat on her bed, his hands covering his face and wept streams and streams of tears ran down his brow to his chest.

Linda's fury began to melt. She had never seen him in tears. So after all, Benito was human? He had told her he had grown up in a place where crying was outlawed by men as by women. That was so, for a society at war could not afford the luxury of crying. People ingested tears and sorrow, and masked their emotions with something more austere than cold blandness, a kind of unspeakable sorrow on a tough cold skin. It was ugly, this sorrow! That was his childhood!

However it happened, he had lost his entire family - father, mother and his two brothers. He was alone in this lonely world, full of absurd problems. The only relative she knew was the baby in her womb, whose life he was about to snuff out a while earlier. His only friend was herself, the mother of his unborn child. Slowly, she moved her hand towards him…

"We must move from here and quickly," Benito said to Linda, the next day. "What about a transfer?"

"I'm almost due one," she replied. "When they posted me here, they said I could apply for a transfer after two years. We are almost there."

"Write an application," said Benito, "get the headmaster to approve it on health grounds and I will take it to the provincial education officer. I'll get it approved there."

The headmaster, Gustavo Machissa, was like a father to Linda. He understood, but wondered how she would fare without his supportive advice and care. He endorsed the request for a transfer with alacrity, but sounded a cautionary 'if a suitable replacement can be found.'

"I will let you go because, when a girl outgrows 'who's the father?' the question becomes 'who's the husband?' I do not want to be a stumbling block to that course of nature."

Two days later, Benito appeared at the provincial education office and was asked to see Senhor Luciano de Carrasco, the man in charge of personnel. "What is it about?" asked the secretary, a bespectacled career civil servant in her late thirties, who, in the words of the cynic, 'could very well pass for forty-three at dusk, with a light behind her.'

Benito passed the letter to her and stepped back. It was the standard procedure.

"Is it official?" the secretary asked.

"Yes, it is," Benito said.

"Then I have to open it," she said, opening. "Then it has to go for registration," she added gratuitously, "and after that it will be filed in your … Are you Emilinda da Vila?"

"No, she is a relative," he said.

"Your sister or your wife?" the secretary asked.

"Yes," Benito said.

"Yes, what? Sister or wife?" the secretary asked.

"Wife is not a relative," Benito said.

"Sister, then?" the secretary said.

"Not quite; my girlfriend," Benito answered.

She lowered her spectacles so she could look at him over the rim. "A girlfriend, a relative?" She looked around the room for the approval of her question by the waiting visitors. Everyone smiled in approval. Benito was embarrassed, but calm.

"Anyway," resumed the secretary, "it has to be filed in her personal file, if it can be located quickly, and then it will join the pile over here," she concluded, tapping the heap of files on the *In Tray*.

"Will all that happen today?" asked Benito, sensing the danger of bureaucratic inordinate delay. "I have come a long way."

"Oh, yes, it will," replied the secretary. "We move quite rapidly here, thank God, especially when people don't keep on asking unnecessary questions and let us get on with our work. You may take a walk around our lovely 'cidade ' and come back at two o'clock. Oh, by the way, do you want to see the chef about the letter or about her?"

"Both, if he won't mind," replied Benito.

"In that case, come back at two-thirty, will you?" she directed, adjusting her glasses.

That afternoon, Benito could not meet Senhor Luciano de Carrasco, evidently because the file had not been 'located.' The next morning, he was told Senhor Luciano de Carrasco would not attend persons until later in the day. He had to settle for the afternoon. That afternoon, de Carrasco 'saw' a lot of people and would probably have seen Benito if a call had not come in from the director, requiring him to proceed with all due haste to the director's office located in another building across the street.

Benito approached the secretary with an earnest appeal. "You see, I'm not from here," he said, "I'm from Culamawe, a long way off."

"Listen, Mr..." she started.

"Benito," he said.

"Listen, Benito. I shouldn't even be talking to you. You are not a member of our staff. Your job ended when you presented the letter from a member of our staff. She knows or should know how we deal with matters here. And being the boyfriend of one of us does not improve anything. I'm only trying to help you because you seem to be a gentleman, albeit a young one. All these files are for people who are out there in the districts. Look at them,

Chiúta, Angónia, Zumbu, Changara, Marávia, Magõé, you see! Come tomorrow and I'll see what I can do."

So, on the third day at 10.45 Benito was ushered into the office of Senhor Luciano de Carrasco. "I understand that you are the boyfriend of one of our teachers, Senhor...?"

"Benito," he introduced himself.

"Yes, Benito?" the director said.

"Is that in the file?" Benito asked.

"No, my friend, I had a little briefing because, you will see, we don't normally deal with strangers about these matters. But yours is a peculiar case, I would say. Yes, indeed, it is not in the file. Now then, Culamawe; unfortunately I have not had occasion to visit the area in eh, eh, but a day will come when an opportunity might present itself. Now, regarding the request that eh... Emilinda da Vila has made, I see it has the endorsement of eh, eh, Gustavo Machissa... this is a man I know very well, a worthy teacher he is, in fact, we went to school together, can you believe it?"

"Oh, yes?"

"You have to pass my greetings to him. Yes, regarding the request, I have to say it has come at a very opportune moment, when we are reviewing deployment of teachers, especially to remote rural areas. Well then, that we will do and I promise you - I'm sure I can - to get back to eh, Gustavo as soon as possible. I'm sure you would be happy to hear that Senhor... Benito! Good day!"

"The matter is extremely urgent, sir," pleaded Benito. "I was hoping..."

"That's why I have said I will... I myself, will get back to Gustavo. I have noted that. In fact, I will put this file aside to be dealt with urgently. Good day... and, eh, say hello to my old classmate."

Benito left, his mission failed; well, almost. Luciano de Carrasco seemed to be saying, 'We will hang you, never fear, most politely, most politely,' or some such words that teem with hidden meaning!

Not once did he mention the health issue, the trump card that Benito had sought to play. If the man was not playing the fool, then he was worse, he was evil. He needed a beer, and Kampango Guest House seemed appropriate for the purpose, it was close enough to his in-laws' home.

A friend of his, Gilberto Lúcio, was there with two others from a Charity that was active in the field of AIDS awareness campaigns. From him, Benito learnt that the NGO was constantly looking for field workers. The pay was good, he told him. Benito managed to secure a lot of literature on the issue to study at home together with Linda.

"Eh, pa. You can't live in the bush and expect to develop anything but shrubs," Gilberto said.

"That's why I am here," replied Benito. "We want to come back to civilisation. But you know how it is. One has to have contacts."

"I'll make you a proposition," Gilberto said. "You study these pamphlets and handouts and see me when you are ready. Can you act?"

"I used to be very good at school."

"Well then, cast your mind back to school and develop it along community theatre lines. It would be an added advantage. You must be able to keep the audience entertained even as you drive an important point home. Get it?"

"Yeah" Like, 'why did you place the cup of tea on the chair? Because the tea is so weak, I thought it should rest a little,' or 'I swear I cannot live without my wife.'

'You love her so much?'

'Not that, old fellow! It's because, you see, she is the one with the money.'

"Is that the kind of thing you want, Gilberto?"

"Where I come from in Angónia," said Gilberto, "the fog is sometimes so thick you can barely see yourself. One day, as they left the bank, a pickpocket put his hand into the coat pocket of a farmer, who had just received payment for his potatoes. Unfortunately for the thief, the man felt it and grabbed the thieving hand.

'What do you want from my pocket?' he asked the thief.

The thief smiled broadly and said, 'I'm awfully sorry, Senhor. I thought it was mine. The fog is so thick!'

Benito went back to Linda in high spirits, not because he saw her transfer as coming, but because he saw a new light for both of them in the AIDS awareness campaign.

She received Senhor Carrasco's promises with a pinch of scepticism, but was glad to hear that her mother, sister and brother were well. Her real pleasure, which she could not even share with Benito, was the literature about HIV/AIDS that he had brought with him. She devoured it like a starved bookworm!

A week later, Senhor Carrasco's response arrived in the form of a summons for her to see the headmaster. She went to his office. "Apparently and unwittingly," he started, as she took a seat in front of him, "I have put my head on the chopping board. He thinks I'm pressurising you to leave. He cannot even consider the possibility until the end of the year. That means another six months."

"By that time I'll be on maternity leave," said Linda.

"That's right. I had underestimated his sense of self-importance. It is not you he is punishing, but I. He wants me to feel his weight, because he could not do that at school. I was then too clever for him. I went into teaching and he went into political manoeuvring. They should have killed him, he would have made a lovely corpse!"

"What a thing to say!" said Linda, shocked.

"Politically speaking, that is," Gustavo Machissa clarified.

"I didn't think he could be that nasty about a simple thing like this," Linda said.

"It is not simple to a small mind locked in a big system. We need better-educated people to handle intricate issues like these. It will take time, but we'll get there. A hunter does not retire all together because he has had an unsuccessful first day in the bush," Machissa said.

"How many unsuccessful days should he think of?" Linda asked.

"A hunter who thinks about quitting before his first buck will never be successful as a hunter," Machissa expounded.

"Then, I'll never make a success at teaching," Linda said.

"Are you thinking of retiring?" Machissa asked.

"If you can call it that," said Linda.

"Are you serious?" Gustavo Machissa asked her.

"Yes," she responded.

"And what do you intend to do with your time?" he asked.

"I will sing, I guess. I have several songs in my heart," she said.

"Well, you better do something about those. A song in the mouth is worth two in the heart," he advised.

"I shall remember that," she said.

"Remember also that time is flying, flying never to return. And don't just fly away; let me know in advance," he told her.

When she got back to her house, Pinto Junior Madeira had just stepped onto her compound. He wore a thin smile that could be deceptive or reassuring, in equal measure. She had met him during certain school functions, where his presence had been sought. He was a short man, who seemed to be convinced that he was tall and, that, in his widely known view, put the matter beyond any argument.

"Good afternoon, Madame Professora," he called out.

"Good afternoon, Senhor Madeira," Linda responded.

"Sorry to come to your house uninvited," he said. "I hope you will excuse me. I'm looking for Benito. Have you seen him?"

"Yes, is there a problem?" she asked.

"No, it's just that I passed by his place and he was not there. Neither him nor Dona Rosa! The neighbours say they have not seen either of them for some time," Madeira said.

"Well, he has been staying here since his mother went to Inhambane to see her people. I wasn't feeling well myself. But he should be at home now. He went there earlier in the day," she told him.

"I must say I'm glad to hear that. We were getting worried, especially in view of the recent sad events. How is he coping?" Madeira asked.

"He is trying, but it has not been easy. I've been trying to encourage him. I hope it works out fine," she said politely.

"Keep it up, Madam. He's a fine young man. Any idea when Dona Rosa might come back?" Madeira asked.

"She was very depressed when I last saw her. I don't know. Might take a while, I guess," she responded despondently.

"Please do remind him that I am always available to discuss matters, if any help is needed," Madeira offered.

"I will tell him," Linda assured the headman.

****

Benito arrived home to find that thieves had been afoot. They had forced the doors open, ransacked the huts and made away with all valuables and clothes. Benito's only remaining clothes were the ones he had soaked in water.

They had then closed the doors and replaced the padlocks so as to deceive the casual passing glance of a passerby.

Benito looked at the empty huts. There stood his mother's hut - the biggest of them, where he spent his early years with his parents and his two brothers. Then there was Araujo's hut, where he spent many happy hours during the first year of Araujo's marriage to Maria, and where he also spent many sad moments with Araujo, during his last days.

His bachelor's hut stood apart, for it was a noisy one, as expected of youthful existence.

The good time was when they were all bustling with activity, with life. Now, they stood empty, derelict, bereft of all warmth. They were tombs without caskets!

He could not even entertain the thought of spending a night there. Where would he sleep?

He moved over to the burial ground, where three graves bearing the remains of his late father and his two brothers stared at him: a stare loaded with unutterable questions.

He had offended them, he knew, but knew not how to appease them. Their spirits would haunt him if he so much as dozed off in this place. It was a haunted place with angry, ethereal ghosts roaming the compound, seeking revenge. Benito retreated step by step, several timid steps. Then he turned and ran…

But he stopped … at the gate. He closed it as noiselessly as he could and left. If there were any ghosts and spirits, as he was convinced there were, he had locked them behind.

Ever since the near-fatal quarrel with Linda, Benito had been searching his heart, his soul and his mind for firm ground to stand on with both legs on the issue of HIV/AIDS. He had carried that debate with him to Tete and he had brought it back to Culamawe, unresolved. Gilberto Lúcio had given him a load of literature on the matter. He had read a lot, enough maybe to satisfy Gilberto, but Linda had read everything.

If his curandeiro was right that the disease was a figment of the Western mind or even an invention of the Western Science, why wasn't there a concerted African response to it? Why hadn't the curandeiros of Africa formulated a traditional doctors' response to the pandemic? Why were their patients dying of the disease? Why did Araujo, who had never used a condom, die from a disease allegedly transmitted through condoms and whose symptoms so squarely fitted those described in the literature that he, Benito, had read?

If the West deliberately introduced HIV/AIDS into Africa, why was the West now spending more money in the fight against it in Africa than all the African nations combined?

He had read somewhere that, in 1997, International Aid had paid 150 million US dollars of the 165 million US dollars spent on HIV/AIDS prevention, the balance being spent mainly by one country: Uganda. Would so much money be spent on fighting a non-existent disease?

Even in the short space of three days he had spent in Tete, he had witnessed two funeral processions of people in high positions who, everyone said, had died of the disease. Was 'everyone' mistaken or was it just a popular rumour, without any basis?

As he turned these questions in his mind, Benito's pace quickened. He wanted to share his ambivalence with Linda.

He arrived at her place to find her deeply worried.

"What's the matter, Linda, my beautiful, beautiful and most beautiful, beautiful and yet again beautiful, Linda?" he asked his girlfriend.

"Stop acting and listen to me," Linda said. "Have you met the headman? He was here a while ago, looking for you."

"Looking for me? What for?" he asked.

"He didn't say. He only said that nobody had seen you for some time. The house had been deserted, he said," Linda responded.

"Is that all?" he asked.

"Yes. I told him you have been staying with me since... since your mother went away, to see her people," she told him.

"And what did he say?" he asked.

"That he was worried about you and hoped you were coping well," she informed him.

"Was he sincere? Did he sound, look, sincere?" he asked.

"I think so, but appearances can be deceptive," she said.

"Did he require me to visit him or did he say he would come back?" Benito asked.

"I told him you had gone to your house," she said.

"Come, Linda. Tell me everything. I want to know everything," he demanded.

That was the beginning of a long discussion, not entirely devoid of argument, that was settled towards midnight by creeping exhaustion and sleep. One decision was taken that was to change their lives. Like the mystery writer they had learnt that it was futile to try to go back, that true life was really going forward, that life was a one-way street and one could never go back. That was a law of nature, just like the force of gravity.

To move forward could never mean to cling to the past: to learn from the past, yes, but not to be held captive by the past. Curandeiros, past or present had, if they faithfully wanted to serve mankind, to learn from the past while embracing the future. To fail to do that, to act to the contrary, especially to teach to the contrary, was a crime against the very society that they served or pretended to serve.

At a time when all medical scientists believe that HIV/AIDS robs the body of its natural defences, the physical mutilation of the body in the name of curative incisions, can only be lumped together with female genital mutilation and other female genital manipulations carried out in Culamawe. Otherwise the outrage is insufficient, inconsequential and irritating!

Benito's curandeiro had said that his ancestors had survived despite the fact that they had never known condoms. True enough, they had, agreed Benito, but at what cost?

His own province was twice the size of Portugal, yet it had only a tenth of the population of Portugal. It was the size of England, but had one-fortieth the population of England. Was it not possible that his ancestors were decimated close to extinction by disease?

"This is not our business, Benito," Linda had said at one point.

"If it isn't our business, whose is it?" he asked her.

"The government, NGOs, United Nations… high level, you know?" she said.

"I don't know. It says here, hear this, Linda. 'The way in which AIDS is still being permitted to gain such a hold on Africa and increasingly Asia, is a human rights question…Many countries in Sub-Saharan Africa are facing the most devastating long-scale development crisis of all time…' You see?" he enlightened her.

"Those are international issues," said Linda. "We need to talk about us. I'm sure Gilberto does not expect you to go and argue your case at the United Nations or the World Health Organisation!"

"Then why did he give me these inflammatory materials?" Benito asked.

"He told you why, didn't he? He told you to prepare to entertain and to inform at the same time. He wants to raise awareness. Don't forget he knows you need to be fired up. Maybe that is why he gave you all the literature. Come, let me hear some suggestions about raising awareness amongst our people," Linda said.

"Ok, the snake that wants to grow up always stays in its hole. Is that good enough?" he asked.

"Try harder, I'm listening," she said.

"How about 'careful is a good way to go'? Would that rub?" he asked again.

"That's close. One more," she said.

"If the music changes, the dance changes too," he said.

"One more," she encouraged.

"When the song ends, the deaf woman continues to dance," he said.

"Just one more!" she begged.

"Prepare now for the solution of tomorrow's problems," he said. He was on a roll.

"I think if you keep it up, you will go a long way," she boosted his confidence.

"And you let me hear yours!" he asked her.

"Tomorrow is pregnant, who knows what it will deliver?" she said.

"And another?" he asked.

"Brooding deepens despair," she said.

"Yes, another," he said.

"As your neighbour speaks, so you reason," she responded.

"One more!" he asked.

"If you do what you should not do, you will see what you should not see," she said.

"And another?" he asked.

"She who swallows a fruit stone has a very high opinion of her throat," she responded.

"Two more!" he cheered.

"Don't be like a shadow: a constant companion, but not a comrade!" she incited.

"And the last one for tonight?" he pleaded.

"There are forty kinds of lunacy, but only one kind of sense," she said.

"And from me, one who takes a light to hunt the whereabouts of a snake should commence at his feet," he said.

"Can you write a short play for each of those sayings?" she asked him.

"I could try, why not? Just use common sense," he said.

"And since common sense was born before the book, let us not shoot the arrow in the dark," she advised.

"It says here that we live in an era of increasing poverty, inequity, institutional ineptitude, war, crime and human rights abuse with globalisation hampering the development efforts of poorer nations. What do you think?" he asked for her opinion.

"Nothing. I'm tired of thinking. I want to sleep," she told him.

"Even about me? Can't you think of something?" he asked.

"I can. I think you are stupid," she said.

"For loving you?" he asked.

"For getting yourself worked up about society," she revealed to him.

"It's not that society I'm worried about, right now. It's you and Junior and me," he said sweetly.

"Then get that job with Gilberto," she said logically.

"That's what I'm gearing up for. I can hear Junior asking me, 'Daddy, what did you do in the Great War; I mean the Third World War?'" Benito said.

"What is your answer?" Linda asked.

"Oh, Junior, I…I let my comrades do the fighting. I did the scheming which was more demanding, though less exciting," he said.

"Why the Third World War?" she asked.

"You see, I fear that the war on HIV/AIDS will escalate and might end up being remembered as the Third World War…with the world pitted against a virus! Not really, but I want to know more about it," he enlightened her.

"I, too, want to know more, much more. I was summoned to see the headmaster this morning after you left. They have refused to transfer me. Your Senhor Carrasco turned out to be a real 'carrasco .' So that makes two of us hunting for a job!" Linda said.

"He looked every other inch a gentleman. But I could see he was a sinister sort under the skin. I have to get back to Gilberto straight away. I've got to get a job. We've got to get out of here," Benito said.

"You have to get out of here first," said Linda, with some emphasis. "It is just a matter of time, is it not? If they should find out…!"

"Linda...stop! That is over and done with, forever. This is Moçambique. We have over two million unexploded anti-personnel landmines scattered all over the country. Even in this area. Nobody ventures into the bush. Nobody will venture there, take it from me," he convinced her.

He paused for a while, moved over to her and held her. "Our lives are inextricably intertwined, Linda. We have to accept that, live with it, die with it. There is no other way. If you can think of one, let me know," he said.

CHAPTER EIGHT

LINDA`S TWINS

Linda was not terribly religious. She doubted that she was even religious. But, like the majority of her countrymen and countrywomen, she had been baptised as a Christian. To that extent, she was religious.

She was religious in another way. Whenever she had a problem, she appealed to God for His intervention. She went to Church only on social occasions, like funeral services, Christmas and baptismal days for close friends, especially friends of her mother, at the latter's insistence and, of course, weddings. In fact, she was of the genre of an average, young Mozambican girl.

In the recent past, she was a much-troubled woman, in her heart, deep down. She had not exhibited any of the known symptoms of infection for an HIV-positive person. She felt entitled to claim that she was HIV negative. But the last visit to the doctor had undermined that confidence, without giving any clear indication of her status. That was a source of great inner remonstrance, inner search, and inner turmoil.

In privacy, she had turned to God and prayed and prayed and prayed each prayer more fervent than the preceding one.

"Hear my prayer, God, for I pray not alone, but with all my heart and the heart of the small wonderful creation that you have seen fit to allow me to carry and to bring into this world, which You Yourself created and bid us to live and to have our being therein. I wail before you God, to save the little one, if it is Your wish that I shall be called mother upon this land. In Your name, I pray. If there be power in prayer, as ordained by You through your Son Jesus Christ, then hear and heed my prayer, O God Almighty."

Every day she prayed, everyday she turned to God, everyday she became more religious, each day a more devout believer than on the previous one.

Recently, she had encountered a scary problem. She had been tracing the small growth in her stomach and felt as if there were two growths instead of one. She had panicked, but could not tell Benito. She thought something had gone wrong, that the growth was disintegrating. Supposing it was all a mere swelling, totally unrelated to pregnancy? Supposing it was a tumour?

But what kind of tumour was it? A doctor had confirmed this one as a pregnancy. True, he had not labelled it a one-embryo pregnancy, but he had said it was a pregnancy. Supposing there were twins growing in there?

With each day her appetite was growing twofold. Could that be the reason?

"O God," she prayed, "don't feed these two to HIV/AIDS, I beseech You! Save them for yourself and for me."

One day she prayed so much that she burst out into tears: and then, slowly into laughter. Maybe even God could get bored with too much prayer!

She remembered a joke she had heard from an Indian shopkeeper in Tete. An Indian, of the turban-wearing Sikh community, had gone to England, studied law and eventually had become a judge. He was presiding over a case in which an old English woman had been accused of shoplifting. The old woman was not expecting justice, let alone mercy, from an Indian judge in a 'bandaged' head. It turned out to be a Daniel come to judgment! He acquitted her and ordered that she be paid ten pound sterling for inconvenience.

'Oh, thank you, my lord,' said the old woman kneeling to the judge. 'Thank you very much, and I hope your head gets better very soon!'

Benito's interview went very well, indeed. He astonished even the sceptical Maputo boss, who seemed to think that nothing good could come out of the Culamawe bushes. Benito was so eloquent that the panel decided to share a bit of its experience with him.

It had happened during oral examinations. The examiner had asked a student a question but, instead of answering, the student had just looked at the examiner.

'It seems to me,' said the examiner, 'that you are very embarrassed by my question!'

'No, sir,' replied the student. 'On the contrary, what really embarrasses me is my answer to your question.'

'And what is your answer?'

'My answer is what makes you think that I should know?'

"Had you been the examiner, Benito," asked the chairman, "what would you have done?"

"I would have let it pass!" Benito said.

He got the job immediately. They needed his calibre.

With a U.S $200 monthly pay package for the next three years, Benito had been catapulted into the world of the working classes. That excluded food and accommodation allowance for the frequent overnight stays in Angónia. That was the news that he brought home to his broadly smiling Linda.

A week later, the pair was packing their personal belongings for the Moatize town, the once prosperous but now rundown railway terminus town, 600 kilometres west of the port city of Beira.

If you have never known what destruction war is capable of inflicting on industry and development, pay a one-day visit to the moribund Moatize Railway Station. You will be depressed for months to come! One hopes that a time will come when that graveyard of derailed and mangled train engines and rusty wagons will be cleared and the Beira Train will sound its whistle again!

One hopes, too, that the tombstone of the halted civil war will never again be lifted, that a fitting epitaph will forever be: 'Here lies the last of the civil wars in this land, dead, embalmed, cremated and buried; never to rise or breathe again.'

Peace, like war, has its own renowned victory, more preferable, more lasting than war.

Tete was a problem town; in as far as accommodation could be a problem. The infrastructure may have been sufficient for a population of forty thousand. It was home to over one hundred thousand, and people were still coming. There was a shortage of every imaginable amenity and an abundance of need.

The decline of Moatize drove away the populace, leaving behind empty houses, upon which looters descended, stripping the houses to mere shells, unfit even for rats but good enough for the cobweb builders!

With the coming of peace, came the returnees and others seeking a roof over their heads. Tete's bursting seams added to the stream of roof-over-head seekers to Moatize. Benito and Linda joined this stream at its height. They settled in Moatize, Baírro de Josina Machel.

Two, not entirely unrelated, problems plagued Moatize at that time. One could be remedied, and could also in time be remedied. It was the incessant water shortage.

The other is a permanent feature of the low-lying hill-ringed urban centre-cum-town. It is sitting on a vast coalfield! When the sun sets after a hard day's toil baking the coal-black soils of Moatize, the power-conserving coals underneath start emitting waves upon waves of nocturnal heat, driving hordes of sweating inhabitants out of their rooms to sleep on the verandas still sweating, but perhaps, less than in the rooms. That is Moatize for you if you open only one eye!

Just to give you an idea.

'Do you know that lady, dear friend?'

'That lady? Oh, wait. Let me see. Oh, yes, I think so. The dress is my wife's. The goggles are those of my daughter. The hat is that of my sister, and the face, yes, the face is that of my housegirl!'

And this.

A fellow hastily filled his pockets with cakes, assuming that nobody was watching him. Then, suddenly, he felt his thigh being scalded with a hot liquid. Upon turning, he saw a colleague pouring tea into his left trouser pocket.

'What the hell do you think you are doing?' he shouted at the colleague.

'Oh, sorry,' responded his colleague respectfully. 'When I saw you taking the cakes and putting them in your pocket, I thought you might need the tea as well!'

Fortunately for Benito and Linda, Moatize was not as sensitive as Tete. Linda was used to Tete and its love of make-believe. People talked as if they lived on rice and chicken, fish and chips, beef-steak and mashed potatoes, squid, prawns and goat meat, and despised those others who lived on pap, sweet potatoes, matapa and 'a certain inferior race of fish' found in the Zambezi River.

The Moatize dwellers were more tactful. They ate pap, sweet potatoes, matapa and that 'inferior race of fish' only on special occasions, like when there was drought or floods and also once in a blue moon!

Otherwise all things being equal or otherwise, they ate rice, chicken, steak, et cetera.

"Can you imagine eating cabbages in your dinner?"

"Do you see what I mean? How can one eat beans and cassava leaves in the evening?"

"Not so loud, Dona Aniceta. I think they are going to cook matapa again. Can you imagine five days of matapa and this, matapa and that? Oh, life must be terribly depressing!"

"If I remember correctly, they had tiger fish two nights away. I couldn't eat until nine at night. It kills my appetite dead!"

"It's murder, I tell you. Anyway, let me check on my prawns. Otherwise, my husband will hit the roof and with reason!"

Giant cockroaches and mosquitoes competed for attention at night while flies stole the limelight by day. Survival entailed constant surveillance with occasional skirmishes. It was from this Vila de Moatize that Benito commuted every working day to Tete.

"Benito, I have to remind you that I'm due for the checkup," Linda said one morning.

He had been too busy arranging his affairs and working on his project to focus on a trivial matter like that. He could follow the progress of the baby's growth without a doctor having to report to him after a few minutes' examination. He, Benito, examined the position every night!

But now he remembered, and was none too happy, that this was the doctor who had thrown doubt as to her status, as to his status. Should they go back to him?

Another British Charity, the Marie Stopes International, had opened a clinic in Tete that provided reproductive health services to the community free of charge and offered other medical services at a minimal fee. Benito proposed a visit to that clinic.

"Do they also carry out testing?" Linda asked.

"Yes, and also counselling," Benito said.

"That is the place for us," Linda agreed.

Benito went off to work. But that day, whatever he touched went wrong. Gilberto, who was his immediate boss, had to intervene several times.

"Eh, pa! What's the problem? Have you forgotten your memory at home or what?" Gilberto asked at one point.

"I'm sorry," Benito replied.

"Don't forget you are on probation," Gilberto reminded him. "Is there something I can do?"

"No," said Benito, "not now."

"Whenever you are ready," said Gilberto, "but be quick. I don't want any blame to be placed on my shoulders. Remember it was my recommendation in the first place!"

Benito's problem was understandable enough, if you knew what it was. But it was not easy for him to disclose, especially to his employer.

Linda's doctor, or rather the doctor she had seen at the hospital, had said that he wanted to see him. That was the same doctor who had hinted that Linda might be infected, without having the courtesy to shed any real light on the suggestion.

Benito had not noticed anything to suggest that Linda was anything but healthy. He had also listened to the vibes in his body and felt robust enough, save for the occasional normal pains.

But supposing he was HIV positive? Supposing Linda was HIV positive? And supposing his unborn son was HIV positive. What a tragedy that would be! They would all perish in the space of…He stopped abruptly. Those were not the thoughts of a normal man.

He turned to God. What had he done to God? He had lost everything already. Why rob him of the only two precious possessions he had left?

He had been careless once, twice or maybe three times. Could one go through life without making a simple mistake? Was it possible for a young man or woman to swim through the shark-infested waters of youth without slipping? And even if they slipped, could God have willed that every such slip be punished by death-slow, ugly, painful death?

Yet, he feared that a finding, a definite test result, that he carried the deadly virus would ruin him and the family that he was attempting to build. His career would be ruined, Linda would become unemployable and the chances of the little one surviving beyond babyhood would be reduced to nil.

But what was preferable; to know or to live with doubt?

Benito opted for early truth; knowledge is power, he mused. After all, that was one of the aims of the organisation he worked for -to encourage voluntary counselling and testing. Would Linda go along with this idea?

Linda did not object; she had already made up her mind. It was absolutely necessary for her to be certain, one way or another. It was better to know how to live with a disease than having to guess.

That did not mean that she was not tormented by the very thought of it. What would happen to her unborn ones? What future would they have? Was God so angry that he could not hear and heed her prayers? Would she not forgive Him if she were Him and He were her?

She held Benito close to her and pressed herself against him.

"I think they are two, Beni," she said softly.

"I wish it were so," he replied, running his hand over her tummy.

"They are not walking about, silly!" she said.

"Oh, so how am I to know?" he asked.

"Press here and here," she said, guiding his hand.

"I can't wait to find out!" said Benito. "Yes, they are two, I swear!"

They appeared at the clinic hand in hand even though their thoughts were not as synchronised. Benito was proud to be the boyfriend of such a beautiful woman and the father of her twins. Linda was happy to be the girlfriend of such a handsome young man, but she would have been happier if she were the wife and not merely his girlfriend. What kind of message were they sending out? That living together was the in-thing?

They approached the reception counter. The receptionist smiled at them. They smiled back at her. Everything appeared to be fine.

"You must be new clients, I guess," the receptionist said kindly. "I know most of the regular clients."

"Oh, yes," said Benito.

"Fill this card for me, will you?" the receptionist requested.

"We need two cards," said Linda.

"Okay. So both of you need help?" the receptionist asked.

"Yes," they said.

"Two cards, then," she said as she handed them the cards.

They were given the cards and they filled them up. Linda sought a pregnancy test to determine how many babies she was expecting and also testing for HIV. Benito sought to have his HIV status established.

"Just take seats and wait," said the receptionist as she took the cards. "Somebody will come for you."

It sounded like 'the devil will come for you'.

For a moment, gloom settled between them, like visitors with a patient in the intensive care unit. Their eyes strayed to the posters on the wall, stopping long enough to note something, but not really reading them. They then turned as by conspiracy and their eyes met.

"Try thinking of love or something," Benito whispered to Linda.

She took his hand into hers.

"Come this way, please!" The voice was unmistakably called in their direction. They turned, rose and followed the neatly dressed nurse into a small, spotlessly clean examination room. It had a bench long enough to hold three, a small table and a chair, actually a stool.

"Please take a seat," she said, pointing to the bench.

They complied and she went into the next room.

On the wall opposite, there was a small poster with a picture of a man chasing a leopard. The caption read: It is the owner of the garden that chases away the leopard, not someone else.

On another poster were the words: Love is the noblest frailty of the mind.

On the third one was the message: 'Tis chastity, my brother, chastity. She that has that is clad in complete steel.'

The nurse came back, closed the door and sat on the stool on the other side of the table, holding a notebook. "You have done the right thing to come together," she said. "It is exemplary and very encouraging. My name is…"

The counselling went very well, with both clients candidly expressing their hopes and fears and expectations, depending on the outcome of the proposed tests. They loved each other very much and were determined to continue with their romance forever.

The counsellor emphasised that the results would be treated with maximum confidentiality and could be revealed to each of them individually, if they so wished.

Were they still willing to go on with the tests?

Yes, they were.

"Would you like to work in this field, to sensitise the rest of society, especially the youth, if such a chance arose?" the nurse asked.

"Oh, yes, very much," replied the couple, simultaneously, as if they had rehearsed.

The nurse took note of that and also took Linda's qualifications. The tests were done and they were asked to come back two weeks later for the results. Then the pair left, hand in hand.

"How do you feel?" Benito asked Linda, when they were out in the Avenida 25 Junho.

"I feel like it's the best thing I've done with my life," Linda responded.

"Me too!" Benito said.

Their waiting game had also begun in earnest. But idleness had to be banished. How does one banish idleness?

Benito tried to get Linda a job with his employer. She was interviewed and passed very well. Unfortunately for her, another lady from Maputo had also passed very well. The latter got the job. The director was from Maputo!

Next, Benito went to the local district education office and the director was very keen to engage Linda in his office as a trainee personnel officer. The provincial office had other ideas. A suitable officer would be sent by the provincial officer as and when it became financially feasible to do so. In fact, a month later, his cousin arrived to take up the post. She was the 'suitable officer' and so it had become financially feasible to engage her.

By this time, however, lady luck had smiled in another way and Linda did not need that job.

Three days before they were to return for the results, a fierce fire had swept through the lower part of Culamawe, rendering the entire forest bare. The fire was fed by strong dry winds that plagued the province annually in August and September. Since there were no fire fighters in the province, as indeed in most parts of the country, the fire raged westwards until it came to the banks of the meandering Zambezi River and, lacking an ally to cross the wide river, shied away and withdrew its hungry flames. Dona Rosa's ashes were scattered all over the land!

The torrential rains and the floods that were to follow in October-November that year, delivered her bones to the Zambezi and on to the Indian Ocean! The floods were to cut off Culamawe from the rest of the world, pound the ground to a bog, swell the streams and leave in their wake devastation, destruction and ruin. Culamawe soon looked like the victim of a vicious gang rape, afraid to look, even heavenward!

How many other Dona Rosas has superstition and witchcraft fed to the hungry crocodiles of the Shirè, Savé, Lúrio, Ruvuma, Limpopo and the Zambezi?

Benito and Linda listened to the radio coverage of the fire and looked at one another, each not knowing what the other was thinking. Benito was thinking about her clothes - they must have been reduced to ashes. Linda was thinking, 'her body must lie exposed now!'

Benito held her hand. "You know, Linda, if I had wealth, I would have flown with you to a more agreeable part of the world, for I hate to see you so sad. But I have been faithful to you Linda, and will always be, even if only in my fashion. I don't know what awaits you or me on Friday, when we go for the results. It does not matter one little hair to me. You might decide otherwise because, unlike me, you have other people. You have a home where, if you were to show up, they would have to take you in. Unlucky me,

I do not have such a home. My home is here, these hands of mine and this head of mine. My home is your home, the reverse befuddles me. Linda, my beautiful Linda, whatever I have is yours, I pledge you that. It may amount to nothing or, indeed, it may amount to a lot, it is yours."

"But…" Linda started.

"Never mind the why, Linda," Benito interrupted her.

"But, I…hunger…" she said.

"Oh, yes. Hunger - a highly indelicate matter! What of it?" Benito cut her short.

"I hunger for you Benito!" she said.

"Will you marry me then?" he proposed.

"Yes, yes, yes!" she said excitedly.

They hugged, kissed, hugged and gazed at each other fixedly, their eyes wet. After long moments of mutual longing and mutual hunger, they kissed yet again and again gazed at each other.

Then Benito reached into his pocket and took out a ring. "This ring I was given by someone I loved just as I love you. Araujo gave it to me. I give it to you." He kissed it and slipped it into her finger. "It is my engagement ring to you." Linda was in tears as he kissed her yet again.

It reminded her of the gravely ill man who, feeling as if his time had come, summoned a lawyer and two witnesses. 'I would like to make my last will and testament,' he told them. 'Firstly, my brother Festo, who has never treated me with respect, I leave nothing at all.'

'All right,' said the lawyer. 'And your other brothers and sisters?'

'To them I also leave nothing.'

'Ah! And what is the motive for so doing?' asked the lawyer, surprised.

'Because I have nothing to my name!'

'Nothing absolutely?'

'Absolutely nothing!'

'So why make the will?'

'I don't want them to fight for nothing!'

Hand in hand they entered the counselling room. It was Friday, their date with fate.

Even as he sat there, waiting, Benito could not but think of all those wasted years, in Culamawe, wasted because they saved no one for him, neither his father nor his mother, nor brothers. They were years of meaningless life. And now, now that he had found the source of real joy, the foundation of an upright, useful life, untainted by hatred and evil scheming, now that he had Linda and her sweet burden with him, all was about to be lost, if... Is that what they meant, that man's life was solitary, poor, nasty, brutish and short?

No, God! Give us a chance! Amen!

Linda's hand strayed and touched his. He almost jumped with fright. "What's the matter?" she asked. "What are you thinking about?"

"About you," he replied.

"Oh, I thought you were scared!" she said.

"No, are you?" he asked.

The door opened and the counsellor came into the room. As usual, she was smiling, the official smile, the trademark smile that revealed little, while concealing volumes and fortunes, lost or won.

By the time she got to the middle of the room, there was a discreet cough at the door and then a short, bespectacled man in a white coat and greying hair entered the room. He was the doctor and looked every inch as knowledgeable and mysterious. His balding scalp and the forming lines on his face announced well in advance that he had seen it all, oftentimes right in front of his eyes.

"This is Doctor Rafael," said the nurse. "He will attend to you and when you are through, the director would like to have a word with you, Linda." She left.

Doctor Rafael looked as if he was not yet ready to reveal his findings to anybody; that is what Benito hoped anyway. He sat on the stool, took off his glasses and laid them on the table. Then he reached for his handkerchief, wiped his misty eyes and put it back in the coat pocket. He touched his stethoscope and, finding it there, took it off his neck and laid it beside his glasses. He rubbed his hands together.

It was combat time, it seemed, and he did not want to incommode himself with nonessentials!

"Life is a trial of strength," he began, without looking at the couple. "Some begin weak and become strong, while others begin strong and become weak. In this particular matter, with this particular disease, none can claim to be strong, although some may claim not to be weak…"

Benito coughed a little. He felt as if he was about to take a large dose of nasty medication. Linda glanced at him, her hand moving closer to his.

"Either way," the doctor said, "all must fight or else all will be lost. Unfortunately, and I know this will come to you, as a major disappointment. There is only one pregnancy, one embryo of a boy child, and not two. The size of the baby may have led you to believe otherwise."

A wave of uncertainty, fright and then calm had swept through the two lovers as he spoke.

"That is the result and I suppose you will not grieve unduly about that," continued the doctor. "Now, the second issue is more complex, as I said earlier. It will demand of you strength and commitment and also good luck…"

He shifted in the small stool and then, as if that was the cue, Benito and Linda adjusted their own positions on the bench. It seemed as if one or both of them were sitting on the edge of the bench with only one buttock! Suddenly, the room felt hot and stuffy!

"We live in a society which is at the cross-roads, without any functional traffic lights. Everybody is seeing green lights even when the lights are red. The amber light appears to have become invisible to all. Nobody blows horns anymore and those who flash their lights are taken to be only saluting. That is the reality, our reality. Remember that and stay on the lookout!" He looked at both of them, put on his glasses and lifted his stethoscope. "You were free of the virus as at the date of your test. The future depends on you. You may go."

A smile appeared on Benito's face, an infectious little smile. That smile soon kindled another smile on Linda's lovely face. Their contagious smiles spread to Doctor Lúcio who, for the first time, smiled … broadly!

About the Author

This Kenyan author writes Novels, Poems, Short Stories and School Readers and has published with EA Literature Bureau, Hodder Education and Cambridge University Press.

Other eBooks by this Author

Set Her Free
Murder In The Rain
Hear Me Angry God
Masai Mara Adventures With Olê Ntutu
The Day Crocodile Wept
The Suitors of Chiuta
Watch Your Mouth
Thank You Grandma
Whispers At Dawn (Poetry)
Returning the Knife
Harvest Festival
Cattle- (Non-fiction)
From the Roaring to the Crouching Lion
My Lovely Elizabeth
Jaws of Justice
Co-authored
Of Friends, Money & Gossip
Great African Women

Printed in the United States
By Bookmasters